Exercises in Style

EXERCISES IN STYLE
by Raymond Queneau

Translated by Barbara Wright
with new exercises translated by Chris Clarke

and exercises in homage to Queneau
by Jesse Ball, Blake Butler, Amelia Gray,
Shane Jones, Jonathan Lethem, Ben Marcus,
Harry Mathews, Lynne Tillman, Frederic Tuten,
and Enrique Vila-Matas

A NEW DIRECTIONS BOOK

New Directions would like to thank the following authors for providing this edition with these new exercises: "Instructions" by Jesse Ball, "Doppelgängers" by Blake Butler, "Viscera" by Amelia Gray, "Assistance" by Shane Jones, "Cyberpunk" by Jonathan Lethem, "Nothing" by Ben Marcus, "Fur Zeu Frentch" by Harry Mathews, "Contingency" by Lynne Tillman, "Beat" by Frederic Tuten, and "Metaliterario" by Enrique Vila-Matas, translated by Anne McLean. These works are protected by copyright, and any request to use this material should be sent to the authors c/o New Directions.

First published in France as *Exercices de style* in 1947 by Editions Gallimard.
Additional exercises from Raymond Queneau, *Œuvres complètes III*, appear in English for the first time by permission of Editions Gallimard.
The music on page 108 is by Pierre Phillipe and is in his handwriting.
The manuscript facsimile on page 184 ("La fonction $\int V(2)_{02}$") is copyright © 2006 by Editions Gallimard and is reproduced by permission.
Initials for the 1958 edition and the permutation of the author's photograph are by Stephen Themerson. Initials for the new exercises are by Barbara Epler.

Manufactured in the United States of America
New Directions Books are printed on acid-free paper.
First published as a New Directions Paperbook (NDP513) in 1981.
This augmented, alternative edition was published as NDP1240 in 2012.

Library of Congress Cataloging-in-Publication Data
Queneau, Raymond, 1903–1976.
[Exercices de style. English]
Exercises in style / Raymond Queneau ; translated by Barbara Wright.
p. cm.
Reissue, with additions, of Wright's 1981 translation of the 1st ed. (1947) of Exercices de style.
Includes bibliographical references.
ISBN 978-0-8112-2035-4
I. Wright, Barbara, 1915–2009. II. Title.
PQ2633.U43E93 2012
843'.914—dc22

2012023824

10 9 8 7 6 5 4 3 2 1

New Directions Books are published for James Laughlin
by New Directions Publishing Corporation
80 Eighth Avenue, New York 10011

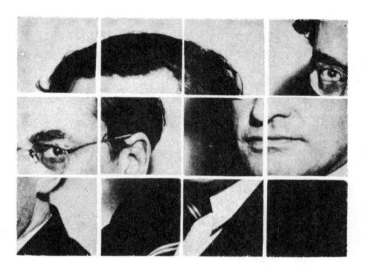

1231
2312
3123

see: permutations, pages 113–117

CONTENTS

MORE EXERCISES IN STYLE
BY RAYMOND QUENEAU

QUENEAU'S 1973 SUBSTITUTIONS

EXERCISES PUBLISHED OUTSIDE OF *EXERCICES DE STYLE*

UNPUBLISHED EXERCISES

EXERCISES IN HOMAGE
TO RAYMOND QUENEAU

PREFACE

Ladies and Gentlemen:[*]

From time to time people politely ask me what I am translating now.

So I say : a book by Raymond Queneau.

They usually react to that in one of 3 different ways.

Either they say : that must be difficult.

Or they say : Who's he?

Or they say : Ah.

Of those three reactions, let's take the third—as the fortune-tellers say.

People say : Ah.

By : Ah—they don't mean quite the same as the people who say : Who's he? They mean that they don't know who Queneau is, but that don't much care whether they know or not. However, since, as I said, this sort of conversation is usually polite, they often go on to enquire : What book of his are you translating?

So I say : *Exercices de Style,*

And then, all over again, they say : Ah.

At this point I usually feel it would be a good idea

[*] Based on a talk given in the Gaberbocchus Common Room on April 1st 1958.

to say something about this book, *Exercices de Style*, but as it's rather difficult to know where to begin, if I'm not careful I find that my would-be explanation goes rather like this:

"Oh yes, *you* know, it's the story of a chap who gets into a bus and starts a row with another chap who he thinks keeps treading on his toes on purpose, and Queneau repeats the same story 99 times in a different ways—it's terribly good . . . "

So I've come to the conclusion that it is thus my own fault when these people I have been talking about finally stop saying "Ah" and tell me that it's a pity I always do such odd things. It's not that my wooffly description is inaccurate—there are in fact 99 exercises, they all do tell the same story about a minor brawl in a bus, and they are all written in a different style. But to say that much doesn't explain anything, and the *Exercices* and the idea behind them probably do need some explanation.

In essaying an explanation, or rather, perhaps, a proper description, I have an ally in this gramophone record, which has recently been made in France, of 22 of the 99 *exercices*. It is declaimed and sung by *les Frères Jacques*—who have been likened to the English Goons. You will hear that the record is very funny. I said it was an ally, yet on the other hand it may be an enemy, because it may lead you to think that the *exercices* are just funny and nothing else. I should like to return to this point later, but first I want to say something about the author of the *Exercices*.

Raymond Queneau has written all the books you see here on the table—and others which I haven't been able to get hold of. He is a poet—not just a writer of poetry, but a poet in the wider sense. He is also a scholar and mathematician. He is a member of the

Académie Goncourt (and they have only 10 members, in comparison with the 40 of the Académie Française), and he is one of the top boys of the publishing house of Gallimard. But he is a kind of writer who tends to puzzle people in this country because of his breadth and range—you can't classify him. He is one of the most influential and esteemed people in French literature—but he can write a poem like this:

> Ce soir
> si j'écrivais un poème
> pour la postérité?
>
> fichtre
> la belle idée
>
> je me sens sûr de moi
> j'y vas
> et
>
> à
> la
> postérité
> j'y dis merde et remerde
> et reremerde
>
> drôlement feintée
> la postérité
> qui attendait son poème
>
> ah mais

Queneau, you see, is not limited, and he doesn't take himself over-seriously. He's too wise. He doesn't limit himself to being either serious or frivolous—or even, I might say, to being either a scientist or an artist. He's both. He uses everything that he finds in life for his poetry—and even things that he doesn't find in life, such as a mathematically disappearing dog, or a proud trojan horse who sits in a French bar and drinks gin fizzes with silly humans.* And all this is, I think, the reason why you find people in England who don't know who Queneau is. Two of his novels were published here, by John Lehmann, in English translations, about 10 years ago. They were, I think, not very successful here. Even though the critics thought they were writing favourably about them. I was looking through the reviews of one of them——*Pierrot*—the other day, and this brings me back to what I was saying about Queneau's wit and lightness of touch being possibly misleading—the book's very brilliance seemed to blind the critics to the fact that it was *about* anything. The *New Statesman* wrote: "*Pierrot* is *simply* a light-hearted little fantasy . . .", and *Time & Tide* came down to Parish Magazine style: "This novel is of the kind called 'so very french'. It is all very unassuming and amusing, and most of us enjoy this kind of fun." According to the current way of thinking (or not-thinking), it seems that if we are to enjoy anything then we must not have to think about it, and, conversely, if we are to think about anything, then we mustn't enjoy it. This is a calamitous and idiotic division of functions.

And this, I think, brings me to the *Exercices de Style*. Queneau is a linguist, and he also has a passionate interest in the French language. He has given a lot of thought to one aspect of it—the French language as *actually spoken*. In *Bâtons, Chiffres et Lettres*, he

* *The Trojan Horse & At the Edge of the Forest.* Gaberbocchus

writes: "I consider spoken French to be a different language, a very different language, from written French." And in the same book, he says: "I came to realise that modern written French must free itself from the conventions which still hem it in, (conventions of style, spelling and vocabulary) and then it will soar like a butterfly away from the silk cocoon spun by the grammarians of the 16th century and the poets of the 17th century. It also seemed to me that the first statement of this new language should be made not by describing some popular event in a novel (because people could mistake one's intentions), but, in the same way as the men of the 16th century used the modern languages instead of latin for writing their theological or philosophical treatises, to put some philosophical dissertation into spoken French."

Queneau did in fact "put some philosophical dissertation into spoken French"—Descartes' *Discours de la Méthode*. At least, he says that it was with this idea in mind that he started to write "something which later became a novel called *le Chiendent*." I won't say anything about the correspondence between it and *le Chiendent* now, but this novel, *le Chiendent*, is one of the easiest to read of all Queneau's novels, and also one of the most touching and thought-provoking. It is also almost farcically funny in parts.

This research into language is, of course, carried on in the *Exercices*. You get plenty of variations of the way different people actually speak—casual, noble, slang, feminine, etc. But you may have noticed that the exercise on p.129 starts like this:

JO UN VE UR MI RS SU DI AP RL TE
(that's in French, by the way. The English translation naturally looks quite different:

ED ON TO AY RD WA ID SM YO DA HE

Now please don't think that I'm going to try to persuade you that this is Queneau's idea of how anyone speaks French. You can't really discover 99 different ways of speaking one language. Well, perhaps you can, but you don't find them in the *Exercices*. I have analysed the 99 variations into roughly 7 different groups. The first—different types of speech. Next, different types of written prose. These include the style of a publisher's blurb, of an official letter, the "philosophic" style, and so on. Then there are 5 different poetry styles, and 8 exercises which are character sketches through language—reactionary, biased, abusive, etc. Fifthly there is a large group which experiments with different grammatical and rhetorical forms; sixthly, those which come more or less under the heading of *jargon*, and lastly, all sorts of odds and ends whose classification I'm still arguing about. This group includes the one quoted above, which is called: *permutations by groups of 2, 3, 4 and 5 letters*. Under *jargon* you get, for instance, one variation which tells the story in mathematical terms, one using as many botanical terms as possible, one using greek roots to make new words, and one in dog latin.

All this could be so clever that it could be quite ghastly and perfectly unreadable. But in fact I saw somewhere that *Exercices de Style* is Queneau's best seller among the French public. I have already intimated that however serious his purpose, Queneau is much more likely to write a farce than a pedantic treatise. His purpose here, in the *Exercices*, is, I think, a profound exploration into the possibilities of language. It is an experiment in the philosophy of language. He pushes language around in a multiplicity of directions to see what will happen. As he is a virtuoso of language and likes to amuse himself and

xvi

his readers, he pushes it a bit further than might appear necessary—he exaggerates the various styles into a reductio ad absurdum—ad lib., ad inf., and sometimes, —the final joke—ad nauseam.

I am saying a lot about what *I* think, but Queneau himself has had something to say about it. In a published conversation with Georges Ribemont-Dessaignes, he says: "In *les Exercices de Style*, I started from a real incident, and in the first place I told it 12 times in different ways. Then a year later I did another 12, and finally there were 99. People have tried to see it as an attempt to demolish literature—that was not at all my intention. In any case my intention was merely to produce some exercises; the finished product may possibly act as a kind of rust-remover to literature, help to rid it of some of its scabs. If I have been able to contribute a little to this, then I am very proud, especially if I have done it without boring the reader too much."

That Queneau *has* done this without boring the reader *at all*, is perhaps the most amazing thing about his book. Imagine how boring it might have been— 99 times the same story, and a story which has no point, anyway! I have spent more than a year, off and on, on the English version of the *Exercices*, but I haven't yet found any boredom attached to it. The more I go into each variation, the more I see in it. And the point about the original story having *no* point, is one of *the* points of the book. So much knowledge and comment on life is put into this pointless story. It's also important that it should be the same story all the time. Anybody can—and automatically does—describe different things in different ways. You don't speak poetically to the man in the ticket office at Victoria when you want to ask him for "two third returns, Brighton." Nor, as Jesperson points out, do you say to him: "Would you please sell me two third-class tickets from London to Brighton and back again, and I will pay you the usual fare for such tickets." Queneau's tour-de-force lies in the fact that the simplicity and banality of the material he starts from gives birth to so much.

This brings me to the last thing I want to say, which is about the English version. Queneau told me that the *Exercices* was one of his books which he would like to be translated—(he didn't suggest by whom). At the time I thought he was crazy. I thought that the book was an experiment with the French language as such, and therefore as untranslatable as the smell of garlic in the Paris metro. But I was wrong. In the same way as the story *as such* doesn't matter, the particular language it is written in doesn't matter as such. Perhaps the book is an exercise in communication patterns, whatever their linguistic sounds. And it seems to me that Queneau's attitude of enquiry and examination can, and perhaps should?—be applied to every language, and that is what I have tried to achieve with the English version.

B. W.

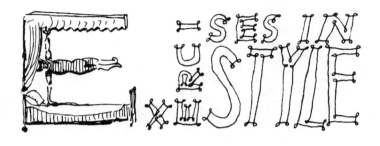

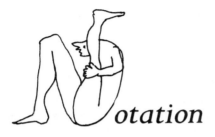

otation

In the S bus, in the rush hour. A chap of about
26, felt hat with a cord instead of a ribbon,
neck too long, as if someone's been having a
tug-of-war with it. People getting off. The
chap in question gets annoyed with one of the
men standing next to him. He accuses him of
jostling him every time anyone goes past. A
snivelling tone which is meant to be aggressive. When he sees a vacant seat he throws
himself on to it.

Two hours later, I meet him in the Cour de
Rome, in front of the gare Saint-Lazare. He's
with a friend who's saying: "You ought to get

3

an extra button put on your overcoat." He
shows him where (at the lapels) and why.

Double Entry

Towards the middle of the day and at midday I happened to be on and got on to the platform and the balcony at the back of an S-line and of a Contrescarpe-Champerret bus and passenger transport vehicle which was packed and to all intents and purposes full. I saw and noticed a young man and an old adolescent who was rather ridiculous and pretty grotesque; thin neck and skinny windpipe, string and cord round his hat and tile. After a scrimmage and scuffle he says and states in a lachrymose and snivelling voice and tone that his neighbour and fellow-traveller is deliberately trying and doing his utmost to push him and obtrude himself on him every time anyone gets off and makes an exit. This having been declared and having spoken he rushes headlong and wends his way towards a vacant and a free place and seat.

Two hours after and a-hundred-and-twenty minutes later, I meet him and see him again in the Cour de Rome and in front of the gare Saint-Lazare. He is with and in the company of a friend and pal who is advising and urging him to have a button and vegetable ivory disc added and sewn on to his overcoat and mantle.

Litotes

Some of us were travelling together. A young man, who didn't look very intelligent, spoke to the man next to him for a few moments, then he went and sat down. Two hours later I met him again; he was with a friend and was talking about clothes.

Metaphorically

In the centre of the day, tossed among the shoal of travelling sardines in a coleopter with a big white carapace, a chicken with a long, featherless neck suddenly harangued one, a peace-abiding one, of their number, and its parlance, moist with protest, was unfolded upon the airs. Then, attracted by a void, the fledgling precipitated itself thereunto.

In a bleak, urban desert, I saw it again that self-same day, drinking the cup of humiliation offered by a lowly button.

Retrograde

You ought to put another button on your overcoat, his friend told him. I met him in the middle of the Cour de Rome, after having left him rushing avidly towards a seat. He had just protested against being pushed by another passenger who, he said, was jostling him every time anyone got off. This scraggy young man was the wearer of a ridiculous hat. This took place on the platform of an S bus which was full that particular midday.

urprises

How tightly packed in we were on that bus platform! And how stupid and ridiculous that young man looked! And what was he doing? Well, if he wasn't actually trying to pick a quarrel with a chap who—so he claimed! the young fop! kept on pushing him! And then he didn't find anything better to do than to rush off and grab a seat which had become free! Instead of leaving it for a lady!

Two hours after, guess whom I met in front of the gare Saint-Lazare! The same fancy-pants! Being given some sartorial advice! By a friend!

You'd never believe it!

10

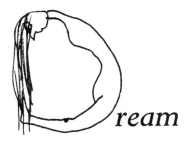

Dream

I had the impression that everything was misty and nacreous around me, with multifarious and indistinct apparitions, amongst whom however was one figure that stood out fairly clearly which was that of a young man whose too-long neck in itself seemed to proclaim the character at once cowardly and quarrelsome of the individual. The ribbon of his hat had been replaced by a piece of plaited string. Later he was having an argument with a person whom I couldn't see and then, as if suddenly afraid, he threw himself into the shadow of a corridor.

Another part of the dream showed him walking in bright sunshine in front of the gare Saint-Lazare. He was with a companion who was saying: "You ought to have another button put on your overcoat."

Whereupon I woke up.

# rognostication

When midday strikes you will be on the rear platform of a bus which will be crammed full of passengers amongst whom you will notice a ridiculous juvenile; skeleton-like neck and no ribbon on his felt hat. He don't be feeling at his ease, poor little chap. He will think that a gentleman is pushing him on purpose every time that people getting on or off pass by. He will tell him so but the gentleman won't deign to answer. And the ridiculous juvenile will be panic-stricken and run away from him in the direction of a vacant seat.

You will see him a little later, in the Cour de

13

Rome in front of the gare Saint-Lazare. A friend will be with him and you will hear these words: "Your overcoat doesn't do up properly; you must have another button put on it."

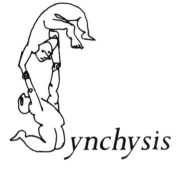

ynchysis

Ridiculous young man, as I was on an S bus
one day chock-full by traction perhaps whose
neck was elongated, round his hat and who
had a cord, I noticed a. Arrogant and snivelling in a tone, who happened to be next to
him, with the man to remonstrate he started.
Because that he pushed him he claimed, time
every that got off anyone. Vacant he sat down
and made a dash towards a seat, having said
this. Rome (Cour de) in the I met him later two
hours to his overcoat a button to add a friend
was advising him.

he rainbow

One day I happened to be on the platform of a violet bus. There was a rather ridiculous young man on it—indigo neck, cord round his hat. All of a sudden he started to remonstrate with a blue man. He charged him in particular, in a green voice, with jostling him every time anybody got off. Having said this, he rushed headlong towards a yellow seat and sat down on it.

Two hours later I saw him in front of an orange-coloured station. He was with a friend who was advising him to have another button put on his red overcoat.

16

Word game

(Dowry, bayonet, enemy, chapel, atmosphere, Bastille, correspondence)

One day I happened to be on the platform of a bus which must no doubt have formed part of the dowry of the daughter of a gentleman called Monsieur Mariage who presided over the destinies of the Paris Passenger Transport Board. There was a young man on this bus who was rather ridiculous, not because he wasn't carrying a bayonet, but because he looked as if he was carrying one when all the time he wasn't carrying one. All of a sudden this young man attacked his enemy—a man

17

standing behind him. He accused him in particular of not behaving as politely as one would in a chapel. Having thus strained the atmosphere, the little squirt went and sat down.

Two hours later I met him two or three kilometres from the Bastille with a friend who was advising him to have an extra button put on his overcoat, an opinion which he could very well have given him by correspondence.

Hesitation

I don't really know where it happened . . . in a church, a dustbin, a charnel-house? A bus, perhaps? There were . . . but what were there, though? Eggs, carpets, radishes? Skeletons? Yes, but with their flesh still round them, and alive. I think that's how it was. People in a bus. But one (or two?) of them was making himself conspicuous, I don't really know in what way. For his megalomania? For his adiposity? For his melancholy? Rather . . . more precisely . . . for his youth, which was embellished by a long . . . nose? chin? thumb? no: neck, and by a strange, strange, strange hat. He started to quarrel, yes, that's right.

with, no doubt, another passenger (man or woman? child or old age pensioner?) This ended, this finished by ending in a commonplace sort of way, probably by the flight of one of the two adversaries.

I rather think that it was the same character I met, but where? In front of a church? in front of a charnel-house? in front of a dustbin? With a friend who must have been talking to him about something, but about what? about what? about what?

recision

In a bus of the S-line, 10 metres long, 3 wide, 6 high, at 3 km. 600 m. from its starting point, loaded with 48 people, at 12.17 p.m., a person of the masculine sex aged 27 years 3 months and 8 days, 1 m. 72 cm. tall and weighing 65 kg. and wearing a hat 35 cm. in height round the crown of which was a ribbon 60 cm. long, interpellated a man aged 48 years 4 months and 3 days, 1 m. 68 cm. tall and weighing 77 kg., by means of 14 words whose enunciation lasted 5 seconds and which alluded to some involuntary displacements of from 15 to 20 mm. Then he went and sat down about 1 m. 10 cm. away.

57 minutes later he was 10 metres away from the suburban entrance to the gare Saint-Lazare and was walking up and down over a distance of 30 m. with a friend aged 28, 1 m. 70 cm. tall and weighing 71 kg. who advised him in 15 words to move by 5 cm. in the direction of the zenith a button which was 3 cm. in diameter.

he subjective side

I was not displeased with my attire this day. I was inaugurating a new, rather sprightly hat, and an overcoat of which I thought most highly. Met X in front of the gare Saint-Lazare who tried to spoil my pleasure by trying to prove that this overcoat is cut too low at the lapels and that I ought to have an extra button on it. At least he didn't dare attack my head-gear.

A bit earlier I had roundly told off a vulgar type who was purposely ill-treating me every time anyone went by getting off or on. This happened in one of those unspeakably foul omnibi which fill up with hoi polloi precisely at those times when I have to consent to use them.

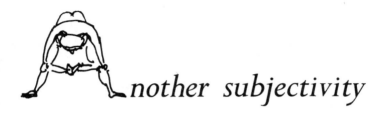

Another subjectivity

Next to me on the bus platform today there was one of those half-baked young fellows, you don't find so many of them these days, thank God, otherwise I should end up by killing one. This particular one, a brat of something like 26 or 30, irritated me particularly not so much because of his great long featherless-turkey's neck as because of the nature of the ribbon round his hat, a ribbon which wasn't much more than a sort of marooncoloured string. Dirty beast! He absolutely disgusted me! As there were a lot of people in our bus at that hour I took advantage of all the pushing and shoving there is every time anyone gets on or off to dig him in the ribs with my elbow. In the end he took to his heels, the milksop, before I could make up my mind to tread on his dogs to teach him a lesson. I could also have told him, just to annoy him, that he needed another button on his overcoat which was cut too low at the lapels.

Narrative

One day at about midday in the Parc Monceau district, on the back platform of a more or less full S bus (now No. 84), I observed a person with a very long neck who was wearing a felt hat which had a plaited cord round it instead of a ribbon. This individual suddenly addressed the man standing next to him, accusing him of purposely treading on his toes every time any passengers got on or off. However he quickly abandoned the dispute and threw himself on to a seat which had become vacant.

Two hours later I saw him in front of the gare Saint-Lazare engaged in earnest conversation with a friend who was advising him to reduce the space between the lapels of his overcoat by getting a competent tailor to raise the top button.

ord-composition

I was plat-bus-forming co-massitudinarily in a
lutetio-meridional space-time and I was neigh-
bouring a longisthmusical plaitroundthehatted
greenhorn.   Who said to a mediocranon:
"You're jostleseeming me." Having ejaculated
this he freeplaced himself voraciously.   In a
posterior spatio-temporality I saw him again;
he was saint-lazaresquaring with an X who was
saying: "You ought to buttonsupplement your
overcoat."   And he whyexplained him.

 *egativities*

It was neither a boat, nor an aeroplane, but a terrestrial means of transport. It was neither the morning, nor the evening, but midday. It was neither a baby, nor an old man, but a young man. It was neither a ribbon, nor a string, but a plaited cord. It was neither a procession, nor a brawl, but a scuffle. It was neither a pleasant person, nor an evil person, but a bad-tempered person. It was neither a truth, nor a lie, but a pretext. It was neither a standing person, nor a recumbent person, but a would-be-seated person.

It was neither the day before, nor the day after,

but the same day. It was neither the gare du Nord, nor the gare du P.-L.-M. but the gare Saint-Lazare. It was neither a relation, nor a stranger, but a friend. It was neither insult, nor ridicule, but sartorial advice.

nimism

A soft, brown hat with a dent in his middle, his brim turned down, a plaited cord round his crown, one hat among many others, jumping only when the bumps in the road were transmitted to him by the wheels of the automobile vehicle which was transporting him (the hat). At each stop the comings and goings of the passengers caused him to make certain lateral movements which at times were fairly pronounced, and this ended by angering him (the hat). He expressed his ire by the intermediary of a human voice which was attached to him by a mass of flesh structurally disposed round a sort of bony sphere perforated by a

32

few holes, which was situated below him (the hat). Then he (the hat) suddenly went and sat down.

One or two hours later I saw him (the hat) again, moving about at roughly 1m. 66cm. above the ground and up and down in front of the gare Saint-Lazare. A friend was advising him to an extra button put on his overcoat . . . an extra button . . . on his overcoat . . . to tell him that . . . him . . . (the hat).

 nagrams

In het S sub in het hurs hour a pach of tabou swinettyx, who had a glon, hint cken and a tah mmitred with a droc instead of a borbin, had an urmagent with athrone gaspenser whom he uccased of stoljing him on sporeup. Having had a good oman he dame a shad orf a feer teas.

An hour trale I emt him in het Cuor ed More, in norft of het rage Tsian-Zalare. He saw with a refind who was yasing to him: "You tough to heav an artex tutnob upt on your oectrova." He woshed him hewer (at het peninog.)

34

istinguo

In an S bus (which is not to be confused with a trespass), I saw (not an eyesore) a chap (not a Bath one) wearing a dark soft hat (and not a hot daft sack), which hat was encircled by a plaited cord (and not by an applauded cat). One of his characteristics (and not his character's instincts) was a prim neck (and not a numb prick). As the people were pushing and shoving (and not the sheep were shooshing and pupping), a newcomer (not a cute number) displaced the latter (not lacerated the display). The chap complained (not the chaplain comped), but seeing a free place (not placing a free See) made a bee-line for it (not

35

bade me lie in for it).

Later I perceived him (not high Erse peeved 'im) in front of the gare Saint-Lazare (and not the lass in Gaza). He was talking to a friend (and not trending to a fork) about a button on his coat (which is not to be confused with a cut on—?—on his boat.)

omeoptotes

On a certain date, a corporate crate on which the electorate congregate when they migrate at a great rate, late, had to accommodate an ornate, tracheate celibate, who started to altercate with a proximate inmate, and ejaculate: "Mate, why do you lacerate, obliterate and excoriate my plates?" But to anticipate Billingsgate debate, he hastened to abdicate, and sate.

An houate aftrate, in front of the Saint-Lazate gate, I notate him agate, talkate about a buttate, a buttate on his overcate.

Official letter

I beg to advise you of the following facts
of which I happened to be the equally
impartial and horrified witness.

Today, at roughly twelve noon, I was present
on the platform of a bus which was proceeding up the rue de Courcelles in the direction
of the Place Champerret. The aforementioned
bus was fully laden - more than fully
laden, I might even ventureto say, since
the conductor had accepted an overload of
several candidates, without valid reason
and actuated by an exaggerated kindness of
heart which caused him to exceed the regu-
lations and which, consequently, bordered
on indulgence. At each stopping place the

perambulations of the outgoing and
incoming passengers did not fail to provoke
a certain disturbance which incited one
of these passengers to protest, though not
without timidity. I should mention that
he went and sat down as and when this
eventuality became possible.

I will append to this short account this
addendum: I had occasion to observe this
passenger some time subsequently in the
company of an individual whom I was unable
to identify. The conversation which they
were exchanging with some animation seemed
to have a bearing on questions of an aesthetic
nature.

In view of these circumstances, I would
request you to be so kind, Sir, as to intimate
to me the inference which I should draw
from these facts and the attitude which you
would then deem appropriate that I adopt
in re the conduct of my subsequent mode of
life.

Anticipating the favour of your reply,
believe me to be, Sir, your very obedient
servant at least.

Blurb

In this new novel, executed with his accus-
tomed *brio*, the famous novelist X, to whom
we are already indebted for so many master-
pieces, has decided to confine himself to very
clear-cut characters who act in an atmosphere
which everybody, both adults and children,
can understand. The plot revolves, then, round
the meeting in a bus of the hero of this story
and of a rather enigmatic character who picks
a quarrel with the first person he meets. In
the final episode we see this mysterious individual listening with the greatest attention
to the advice of a friend, a past master of
Sartorial Art. The whole makes a charming

impression which the novelist X has etched with rare felicity.

nomatopoeia

On the platform, pla pla pla, of a bus, chuff chuff chuff, which was an S (and singing still dost soar, and soaring ever singest), it was about noon, ding dang dong, ding dang dong, a ridiculous ephebus, poof poof, who had one of those hats, pooh, suddenly turned (twirl twirl) on his neighbour angrily, grrh grrh, and said, hm hm: "You are purposely jostling me, Sir," Ha ha. Whereupon, phfftt, he threw himself on to a free seat and sat down, plonk.

The same day, a bit later, ding dang dong, ding dang dong, I saw him again in the company of another ephebus, poof poof, who was talking overcoat buttons, (boorra boorra, it wasn't as warm as all that . . .)

Ha ha.

logical analysis

Bus.
Platform.
Bus platform. That's the place.
Midday.
About.
About midday. That's the time.
Passengers.
Quarrel.
A passengers' quarrel. That's the action.
Young man.
Hat. Long thin neck.
A young man with a hat and a plaited cord
     round it. That's the chief character.
Person.

44

A person.
A person. That's the second character.
Me.
Me.
Me. That's the third character, narrator.
Words.
Words.
Words. That's what was said.
Seat vacant.
Seat taken.
A seat that was vacant and then taken. That's
    the result.
The gare Saint-Lazare.
An hour later.
A friend.
A button.
Another phrase heard. That's the conclusion.
Logical conclusion.

nsistence

One day, at about midday, I got into an S bus which was nearly full. In an S bus which was nearly full there was a rather ridiculous young man. I got into the same bus as he, and this young man, having got into this same nearly full S bus before me, at about 12 noon, was wearing on his head a hat which I found highly ridiculous, I, the person who happened to be in the same bus as he, on the S line, one day, at about 12 noon.

This hat was encircled by a sort of lanyard-like plaited cord, and the young man who was wearing the hat—and the cord—happened to

46

be in the same bus as I, a bus which was nearly full because it was 12 noon; and underneath the hat, whose cord was an imitation of a lanyard, was a face succeeded by a long neck, by a long, long neck. Ah, how long it was, the neck of the young man who was wearing a hat encircled by a lanyard on an S bus, one day at about 12 noon.

There was a lot of pushing and shoving in the bus which was conveying us towards the terminus of the S line, one day at about 12 noon, me and the young man who had put a long neck under a ridiculous hat. The jolts which occurred resulted in a protest, which protest emanated from the young man who had such a long neck on the platform of an S bus, one day at about 12 noon.

There was an accusation formulated in a voice damp with wounded dignity, because on the platform of an S bus, a young man had a hat which was equipped with a lanyard all the way round it, and a long neck; there was also a vacant seat suddenly in this S bus which was nearly full because it was 12 noon, a seat which was soon occupied by the young man with the long neck and the ridiculous hat, a

47

seat which he coveted because he didn't wish to get pushed around any more on that bus platform, one day at about 12 noon.

Two hours later I saw him again in front of the gare Saint-Lazare, the young man whom I had noticed on the platform of an S bus, the same day, at about 12 noon. He was with a companion of the same species as himself who was giving him some advice relative to a certain button on his overcoat. The other was listening attentively. The other—that's the young man who had a lanyard round his hat, and whom I saw on the platform of a nearly full S bus, one day, at about 12 noon.

gnorance

Personally I don't know what they want of me. Yes, I got on an S bus about midday. Were there a lot of people? Of course there were, at that hour. A young man with a felt hat? It's quite possible. Personally I don't examine people under a microscope. I don't give a damn. A kind of plaited cord? Round his hat? I'll agree that's a bit peculiar, but it doesn't strike me personally as anything else. A plaited cord . . . He had words with another man? There's nothing unusual about that.

And then I saw him again an hour or two later? Why not? There are a lot of things in life that are more peculiar than that. For instance, I remember my father was always telling me about . . .

ast

I got into the Porte Champerret bus. There were a lot of people in it, young, old, women, soldiers. I paid for my ticket and then looked around me. It wasn't very interesting. But finally I noticed a young man whose neck I thought was too long. I examined his hat and I observed that instead of a ribbon it had a plaited cord. Every time another passenger got on there was a lot of pushing and shoving. I didn't say anything, but all the same the young man with the long neck started to quarrel with his neighbour. I didn't hear what he said, but they gave each other some dirty looks. Then the young man with the long neck went and sat down in a hurry.

Coming back from the Porte Champerret I passed in front of the gare Saint-Lazare. I saw my young man having a discussion with a pal. the pal indicated a button just above the lapels of the young man's overcoat. Then the bus took me off and I didnt see them any more. I had a seat and I wasn't thinking about anything.

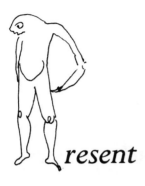 *resent*

At midday the heat coils round the feet of bus passengers. If, placed on a long neck, a stupid head adorned with a grotesque hat should chance to become inflamed, then a quarrel immediately breaks out. Very soon to become dissipated, however, in an atmosphere too heavy to carry ultimate insults very vividly from mouth to ear.

Thus one goes and sits down inside, where it's cool.

Later can be posed, in front of stations with double courtyards, sartorial questions about some button or other which fingers slimy with sweat self-confidently fiddle with.

eported speech

Dr. Queneau said that it had happened at mid-day. Some passengers had got into the bus. They had been squashed tightly together. On his head a young man had been wearing a hat which had been encircled by a plait and not by a ribbon. He had had a long neck. He had complained to the man standing next to him about the continual jostling which the latter had been inflicting on him. As soon as he had noticed a vacant seat, said Dr. Queneau, the young man had rushed off towards it and sat down upon it.

He had seen him later, Dr. Queneau continued,

in front of the gare Saint-Lazare. He had been wearing an overcoat, and a friend who had happened to be present had made a remark to him to the effect that he ought to put an extra button on the said overcoat.

Passive

It was midday. The bus was being got into by passengers. They were being squashed together. A hat was being worn on the head of a young gentleman, which hat was encircled by a plait and not by a ribbon. A long neck was one of the characteristics of the young gentleman. The man standing next to him was being grumbled at by the latter because of the jostling which was being inflicted on him by him. As soon as a vacant seat was espied by the young gentleman it was made the object of his precipitate movements and it became sat down upon.

56

The young gentleman was later seen by me in front of the gare Saint-Lazare. He was clothed in an overcoat and was having a remark made to him by a friend who happened to be there to the effect that it was necessary to have an extra button put on it.

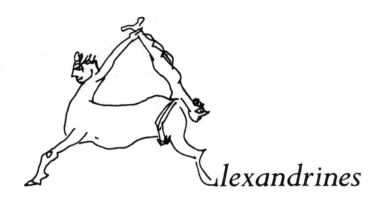

lexandrines

One midday in the bus—the S-line was its ilk—
I saw a little runt, a miserable milk—
Sop, voicing discontent, although around his
    turban
He had a plaited cord, this fancy-pants subur-
    ban.
Now hear what he complained of, this worm-
    metamorphosis
With disproportionate neck, suffering from
    halitosis :
—A citizen standing near him who'd come to
    man's estate
Was constantly refusing to circumnavigate
His toes, each time a chap got in the bus and
    rode,

Panting, and late for lunch, towards his chaste
    abode.
But scandal was there none; this sorry per-
    sonage
Espied a vacant seat—made thither quick
    pilgrimage.
As I was going back towards the Latin Quarter
I saw him once again, this youth of milk-and-
    water.
And heard his foppish friend telling him with
    dispassion :
"The opening of your coat is not the latest
    fashion."

olyptotes

I got into a bus full of taxpayers who were giving some money to a taxpayer who had on his taxpayer's stomach a little box which allowed the other taxpayers to continue their taxpayers' journeys. I noticed in this bus a taxpayer with a long taxpayer's neck and whose taxpayer's head bore a taxpayer's felt hat encircled by a plait the like of which no taxpayer ever wore before. Suddenly the said taxpayer peremptorily addressed a nearby taxpayer, complaining bitterly that he was purposely treading on his taxpayer's toes every time other taxpayers got on or off the taxpayers' bus. Then the angry taxpayer went

60

and sat down in a seat for taxpayers which another taxpayer had just vacated. Some taxpayer's hours later I caught sight of him in the Cour for the taxpayers de Rome, in the company of a taxpayer who was giving him some advice on the elegance of the taxpayer.

 *pheresis*

Ot us sengers. Ticed ung an eck embled at affe ring at ith ted ord. Ot gry nother senger plaining rod oes very one n ut. Ent at own here as ree eat.

Ing ack eft ank ticed king own ith riend ving vice ow egant wing irst ton oat.

 *pocope*

I g into a bu full of passen. I no a yo ma whose n resem th of a gir and who was wea a h w a plai cor. He g an with a passen, complai that he tr on his t e time any got i or o. Then he w and s d because th w a f s.

Go b l b, I no him wal up and d w a f who was gi him ad on h to be ele, sho him the f but of his c.

Syncope

I gt io bs full opssgers. I niced a youngn with a nesemataraffe and with a hathaplord. He got angwer pssger because he comined that he troes. Then he occed a vnt st.

When I was ging along the sroute in the oppection, I niced him in Courome. He was beven a lon in egance weference ta bun.

Speaking personally

That's something I do understand; a chap who goes out of his way to tread on your dogs, it makes you bloody wild. But after you've made a fuss about it to go and sit down like a bloody coward, that personally I don't understand. I saw it with my own eyes the other day on the back platform of an S bus. Personally I thought the young man's neck was somewhat long and I also thought that kind of plait thing round his hat was bloody silly. Personally I would never dare to show myself in such a get-up. But anyway, like I said, when he'd moaned at another passenger who was treading on his toes, this chap went and sat down and that was that. Personally I would have clipped him one, any bastard that trod on my toes.

I tell you, personally I think there are some odd things in this life, it's only mountains that never meet. A couple of hours later I met that young chap again. I saw him with my own eyes in front of the gare Saint-Lazare. Yes, I saw him myself with a friend of his own kidney who was saying—I heard him with my own ears: "You ought to raise that button." I personally saw him with my own eyes, he was pointing to the top button.

Exclamations

Goodness! Twelve o'clock! time for the bus!
what a lot of people! what a lot of people!
aren't we squashed! bloody funny! that chap!
what a face! and what a neck! two-foot long!
at least! and the cord! the cord! I hadn't
seen it! the cord! that's the bloody funniest!
oh! the cord! round his hat! A cord! bloody
funny! too bloody funny! here we go, now
he's yammering! the chap with the cord! at
the chap next to him! what's he saying! The
other chap! claims he trod on his toes!
They're going to come to blows! definitely!
no, though! yes they are, though! go wonn!
go wonn! bite him in the eye! charge! hit

67

'im! well I never! no, though! he's climbing down! the chap! with the long neck! with the cord! it's a vacant seat he's charging! yes! the chap!

Well! 't's true! no! I'm right! it's really him! over there! in the Cour de Rome! in front of the gare Saint-Lazare! mooching up and down! with another chap! and what's the other chap telling him! that he ought to get an extra button! yes! a button on his coat!   On his coat!

You know

Well, *you* know, the bus arrived, so, *you* know, I got on. Then I saw, *you* know, a citizen who, *you know*, caught my eye, sort of. I mean, *you* know, I saw his long neck and I saw the plait round his hat. Then he started to, *you* know, rave, at the chap next to him. He was, *you* know, treading on his toes. Then he went and, *you* know, sat down.

Well, *you* know, later on, I saw him in the Cour de Rome. He was with a, *you* know, pal, and he was telling him, *you* know, the pal was: "You ought to get another button put on your coat." *You* know.

69

oble

At the hour when the rosy fingers of the dawn
start to crack I climbed, rapid as a tongue of
flame, into a bus, mighty of stature and with
cow-like eyes, of the S-line of sinuous course.
I noticed, with the precision and acuity of a
Red Indian on the warpath, the presence of a
young man whose neck was longer than that
of the swift-footed giraffe, and whose felt hat
was adorned with a plait like the hero of an
exercise in style. Baleful Discord with breasts
of soot came with her mouth reeking of a
nothingness of toothpaste, Discord, I say, came
to breathe her malignant virus between this
young man with the giraffe neck and the plait
70

round his hat, and a passenger of irresolute and farinaceous mien. The former addressed himself to the latter in these terms: "I say, you, anyone might think you were treading on my toes on purpose!" Having said these words, the young man with the giraffe neck and the plait round his hat quickly went and sat down.

Later, in the Cour de Rome of majestic proportions, I again caught sight of the young man with the giraffe neck and the plait round his hat, accompanied by a friend, an arbiter elegantiarum, who was uttering these words of censure which I could hear with my agile ear, censure which was directed to the most exterior garment of the young man with the giraffe neck and the plait round his hat: "You ought to diminish its opening by the addition or elevation of a button to or on its circular periphery."

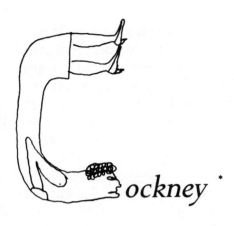

ockney *

So A'm stand'n' n' ahtsoider vis frog bus when A sees vis young Froggy bloke, caw bloimey, A finks, 'f'at ain't ve most funniest look'n' geezer wot ever A claps eyes on. Bleed'n' great neck, jus' loike a tellyscope, strai' up i' was, an' ve titfer 'e go' on 'is bonce, caw, A fought A'd 'a died. Six foot o' skin an' grief, A ses to meself, when awlver sud'n 'e starts to come ve ol' acid, an': "Gaw bloimey," 'e ses, "wot ver ber-lee-din' ow yeh fink yeh adeouin' of?" 'E's tawkin' to annuver bleed'n' fawrner vere on ve bus pla'form; ses 'e keeps a-treadin' on 'is plites awler toime, real narky 'e gets, till vis uvver Frog bloke turns roun' an'

ses : " 'Ere," 'e ses, "oo yeh fink yeh git'n' a'?
Garn," 'e ses, "A'll give yeh a pro'r mahrfful
na minute," 'e ses, "gi' ah a vit." So 'e does,
pore bastard, 'e does a bunk real quick deahn
ve bus wivaht anuvver word.

Cup lowers la'r, guess wo'? A sees ve fust
young bleeder agin walkin' up'n deahn ahtsoider ve Garsn Lazzer, arkin' to anuvver
young Froggy a-jorein' 'im abeaht a bleedin'
bu'en.

* Replacing *Vulgaire*

73

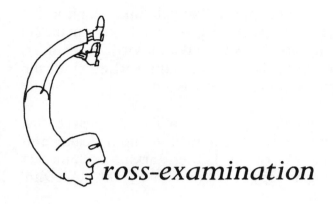

Cross-examination

—At what time did the 12.23 p.m. S-line bus proceeding in the direction of the Porte de Champerret arrive on that day?
—At 12.38 p.m.
—Were there many people on the aforesaid S bus?
—Bags of 'em.
—Did you particularly notice any of them?
—An individual who had a very long neck and a plait round his hat.
—Was his demeanour as singular as his attire and his anatomy?
—At the very beginning, no; it was normal, but in the end it proved to be that of a slightly

hypotonic paranoiac cyclothymic in a state of hypergastric irritability.

—How did that become apparent?

—The individual in question interpellated the man next to him and asked him in a whining tone if he was not making a point of treading on his toes every time any passengers got on or off.

—Had this reproach any foundation?

—I've no idea.

—How did the incident terminate?

—By the precipitate flight of the young man who went to occupy a vacant seat.

—Was there any sequel to this incident?

—Less than two hours later.

—In what did this sequel consist?

—In the reappearance of this person across my path.

—Where and how did you see him again?

—When I was passing the Cour de Rome in a bus.

—What was he doing there?

—He was being given some sartorial advice.

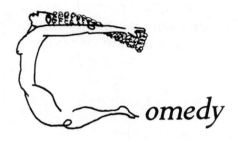 *omedy*

ACT ONE
SCENE 1
On the back platform of an S bus, one day, round about 1 2 noon.

THE CONDUCTOR : Fez pliz. (*Some passengers hand him their fares.*)

SCENE 2
(*The bus stops*)

THE CONDUCTOR : Let 'em off first. Any priorities? One priority! Full up. Dring dring dring.

ACT TWO
SCENE 1

(*Same set.*)

FIRST PASSENGER : (*young, long neck, a plait round his hat*) It seems, Sir, that you make a point of treading on my toes every time anyone goes by.

SECOND PASSENGER : (*shrugs his shoulders*)

SCENE 2

(*A third passenger gets off*)

FIRST PASSENGER: (*to the audience*) Whacko! a free seat! I'll get it before anyone else does. (*He precipitates himself on to it and occupies if*)

ACT THREE
SCENE 1

(*The Cour de Rome*)

A YOUNG DANDY : (*to the first passenger, now a pedestrian*) The opening of your overcoat is too wide. You ought to make it a bit narrower by having the top button raised.

SCENE 2

On the S bus, passing the Cour de Rome.

FOURTH PASSENGER : Huh, the chap who was in the bus with me earlier on and who was

77

having a row with another chap. Odd encounter. I'll make it into a comedy in three acts and in prose.

 *sides*

The bus arrived bulging with passengers. *Only hope I don't miss it, oh good, there's still just room for me.* One of them *queer sort of mug he's got with that enormous neck* was wearing a soft felt hat with a sort of little plait round it instead of a ribbon *just showing off that is* and suddenly started *hey what's got into him* to vituperate his neighbour *the other chap isn't taking any notice of him* reproaching him for deliberately treading *seems as if he's looking for trouble but he'll climb down* on his toes. But as there was a free seat inside *didn't I say so* he turned his back and made haste to occupy it.

About two hours later *coincidences are peculiar* he was in the Cour de Rome with a friend *a fancy-pants of his own sort* who was pointing with his index finger to a button on his overcoat *what on earth can he be telling him?*

 *arechesis*

On the butt-end of a bulging bus which was transbustling an abundance of incubuses and Buchmanites from bumbledom towards their bungalows, a bumptious buckeen whose buttocks were remote from his bust and who was buttired in a boody ridiculous busby, buddenly had a bust-up with a robust buckra who was bumping into him: "Buccaneer, buzz off, you're butting my bunions!" Rebuffed, he did a bunk.

But bussequently I buheld him with a buckish buddy who was busuading him to budge a button on his bum-freezer.

Spectral

We, gamekeeper of the Monceau Plain, have the honour to report the inexplicable and malignant presence in the neighbourhood of the oriental gate of the Park, property of his Royal Highness Monsieur Philippe, the invested Duke of Orleans, this sixteenth day of May one thousand seven hundred and eighty three, of a felt hat of an unwonted shape and encircled by a sort of plaited cord. We subsequently observed the sudden apparition under the said hat of a man who was young, endowed with a neck of an extraordinary length, and dressed how they dress, doubtless, in China. The appalling aspect of this individual froze our blood and prevented our flight. This individual remained immobile for several instants, and then began to make agitated movements, muttering the while, as if pushing aside other individuals in his vicinity who were invisible but perceptible to him. Suddenly he transferred his attention to his cloak and we heard him murmuring as follows : "A button is missing, a button is missing." Then he started to move and took the direction of the Nursery Garden. Attracted in spite of ourself by the strangeness of this phenomenon, we followed him out of the confines attributed to our jurisdiction and we all three, we, the individual and the hat, reached a deserted little garden, which was planted with cabbages. A blue sign of unknown but certainly diabolical origin bore the inscription "Cour de Rome". The individual continued to move about for some moments, murmuring: "He tried to tread on my toes." Then he disappeared, first himself, and, some time after, his hat. Having drawn up a report of this liquidation, I went to have a drink at the Little Poland.

 *hilosophic*

Great cities alone can provide phenomenological spirituality with the essentialities of temporal and improbabilistic coincidences. The philosopher who occasionally ascends into the futile and utilitarian inexistentiality of an S bus can perceive therein with the lucidity of his pineal eye the transitory and faded appearance of a profane consciousness afflicted by the long neck of vanity and the hatly plait of ignorance. This matter, void of true entelechy, occasionally plunges into the categorical imperative of its recriminatory life force against the neo-Berkleyan unreality of a corporeal mechanism unburdened by conscience. This

84

moral attitude then carries the more uncon-
scious of the two towards a void spatiality
where it disintegrates into its primary and
crooked elements.

Philosophical research is then pursued norm-
ally by the fortuitous but anagogic encounter
of the same being accompanied by its inessen-
tial and sartorial replica, which is noumenally
advising it to transpose on the level of the
understanding the concept of overcoat button
situated sociologically too low.

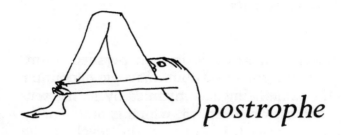

Apostrophe

O platinum-nibbed stylograph, let thy smooth and rapid course trace on this single-side calendered paper those alphabetic glyphs which shall transmit to men of sparkling spectacles the narcissistic tale of a double encounter of omnibusilistic cause. Proud courser of my dreams, faithful camel of my literary exploits, lissome fountain of words counted, weighed and chosen, describe thou those lexicographic and syntactic curves which shall graphically create the futile and ridiculous narration of the life and opinions of that young man who one day took the S bus without suspecting that he would become the immortal hero of the pre-

86

sent writer's laborious toil. O coxcomb with thy plait-girdled hat projecting over thy long neck, O cross-grained, choleric and pusillanimous cur who, fleeing the skirmish, wentest to place thy behind, harvester of kicks on the arse, on a bench of hardened wood, didst thou suspect this thy rhetorical destiny whilst, before the gare Saint-Lazare, thou wast listening with exalted ear to the tailoring counsel of a personage inspired by the uppermost button of thine overcoat?

Awkward

I'm not used to writing. I dunno. I'd quite
like to write a tragedy or a sonnet or an ode,
but there's the rules. They put me off. They
weren't made for amateurs. All this is already
pretty badly written. Oh well. At any rate,
I saw something today which I'd like to set
down in writing. Set down in writing doesn't
seem all that marvellous to me. It's probably
one of those ready-made expressions which are
objected to by the readers who read for the
publishers who are looking for the originality
which they seem to think is necessary in the
manuscripts which the publishers publish
when they've been read by the readers who
88

object to ready-made expressions like "to set down in writing" which all the same is what I should like to do about something I saw today even though I'm only an amateur who is put off by the rules of the tragedy the sonnet or the ode because I'm not used to writing.   Hell, I don't know how I did it but here I am right back at the beginning again.   I'll never get to the end.   So what.   Let's take the bull by the horns. Another platitude. And anyway there was nothing of the bull about that chap.   Huh, that's not bad.   If I were to write : let's take the fancy-pants by the plait of his felt hat which hat is conjugated with a long neck, that might well be original.   That might well get me in with the gentlemen of the French Academy, the Café Flore and the Librairie Gallimard.   Why shouldn't I make some pro-gress, after all. It's by writing that you become a writesmith.   That's a good one.   Have to keep a sense of proportion, though.   The chap on the bus platform had lost his when he started to swear at the man next to him claim-ing that the latter trod on his toes every time he squeezed himself up to let passengers get on or off.   All the more so as after he'd pro-tested in this fashion he went off quickly enough to sit down as soon as he'd spotted a free seat inside as if he was afraid of getting hit. Hm, I've got through half my story already. Wonder how I did it. Writing's really quite pleasant. But there's still the most difficult part left. The part where you need the most know-how. The transition. All the more so as there isn't any transition. I'd rather stop here.

asual

I

I get on the bus.
"Is this right for the Porte Champerret?"
"Cantcher read?"
"Pardon."
He grinds my tickets on his stomach.
"Ee yar."
"Thanks."
I look around me.
"I say, you."
He has a sort of cord round his hat.
"Can't you look what you're doing?"
He has a very long neck.
"Oh look here, I say."

Now he's rushing to get a free seat.
"Well well."
I say that to myself.

II

I get in the bus.
"Is this right for the Place de la Contrescarpe?"
"Cantcher read?"
"Pardon."
His barrel organ functions and gives me back
my tickets with a little tune on them.
"Ee yar.'
"Thanks."
We pass the gare Saint-Lazare.
"Hm, there's the chap I saw before."
I incline an ear.
"You ought to get another button put on your
overcoat."
He shows him where.
"Your overcoat is cut too low."
That's true enough.
"Well well."
I say that to myself.

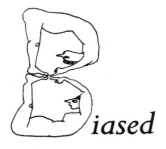

Biased

After an inordinate delay the bus at last turned the corner and pulled up alongside the pavement. A few people got off, a few others got on. I was among the latter. I got shoved on to the platform, the conductor vehemently pulled a noise-plug and the vehicle started off again. While I was engaged in tearing out of a little book the number of tickets that the man with the little box was about to obliterate on his stomach, I started to inspect my neighbours. Nothing but males around me. No women. A disinterested look, then. I soon discovered the cream of this surrounding mud: a boy of about twenty who wore a little head on a long neck and a large hat on his little head and a pretty little plait round his large hat.

What a ghastly type, I said to myself.

He wasn't only a ghastly type, he was a quarrelsome one as well. He worked himself up into a state of indignation and accused a perfectly ordinary citizen of laminating his feet every time a passenger went by getting on or off. The other fellow looked at him severely, trying to find an aggressive retort in the ready-made repertory that he no doubt lugged around with him through the varying circumstances of Life, but he was somewhat out of his depth that day. As for the young man, he was afraid he was going to get his face slapped, so he took advantage of the sudden liberation of a seat by precipitating himself upon it and sitting on it.

I got off before he did and couldn't continue to observe his behaviour. I was deciding to condemn him to oblivion when, two hours later, me in the bus, him on the pavement, I saw him in the Cour de Rome, looking just as deplorable.

94

He was walking up and down in the company of a friend who must have been his arbiter of elegance and who was advising him, with dandyesque pedantry, to reduce the space between the lapels of his overcoat by having a supplementary button united to it.

What a ghastly type, I said to myself.

Then the two of us, my bus and I, continued on our way.

Sonnet

Glabrous was his dial and plaited was his
  bonnet,
And he, a puny colt—(how sad the neck he
  bore,
And long)—was now intent on his quotidian
  chore—
The bus arriving full, of somehow getting on
  it.

One came, a number ten—or else perhaps an S,
Its platform, small adjunct of this plebeian
  carriage,
Was crammed with such a mob as to preclude
  free passage;
Rich bastards lit cigars upon it, to impress.

The young giraffe described so well in my first
    strophe,
Having got on the bus, started at once to curse
    an
Innocent citizen—(he wanted an easy trophy

But got the worst of it.)   Then, spying a vacant
    place,
Escaped thereto. Time passed. On the way
    back, a person
Was telling him that a button was just too
    low in space.

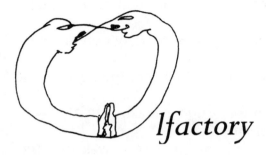 *lfactory*

In that meridian S, apart from the habitual smell, there was a smell of a beastly seedy ego, of effrontery, of jeering, of H-bombs, of a high jakes, of cakes and ale, of emanations, of opium, of curious ardent esquimos, of tumescent venal double-usurers, of extraordinary white zoosperms, there was a certain scent of long juvenile neck, a certain perspiration of plaited cord, a certain pungency of anger, a certain loose and constipated stench, which were so unmistakeable that when I passed the gare Saint-Lazare two hours later I recognised them and identified them in the cosmetic, modish and tailoresque perfume which emanated from a badly placed button.

98

ustatory

This particular bus had a certain taste. Curious, but undeniable. All buses don't have the same taste. That's often said, but it's true. Just try the experiment. This one—an S, not to make too great a mystery of it—had the suspicion of a flavour of grilled peanuts, not to go into too great detail. The platform had its own special bouquet, peanuts not just grilled but trodden as well. One metre 60 above the trampolin, a gourmand, only there wasn't one there, would have been able to taste something rather sourish which was the neck of a man of about thirty. And twenty centimetres higher still, the refined palate was offered the

99

rare opportunity of sampling a plaited cord just slightly tinged with the flavour of cocoa. Next we sampled the chewing gum of dispute, the chestnuts of irritation, the grapes of wrath and a bunch of bitterness.

Two hours later we were entitled to the dessert : an overcoat button . . . a real delicacy.

 *actile*

Buses are soft to the touch especially if you take them between the thighs and caress them with both hands, from the head towards the tail, from the engine towards the platform. But when you find yourself on this platform, then you perceive something rougher and harsher which is the bar or hand-rail, and sometimes something rounder and more elastic which is a buttock. Sometimes there are two of these and then you put the sentence into the plural. You can also take hold of a tubular, palpitating object that disgurgitates idiotic sounds, or even a utensil with plaited spirals that are softer than a rosary, silkier than barbed wire, more velvety than rope, and slenderer than a cable. Or your finger can even touch human clottishness, slightly viscous and gummy on account of the heat.

Then if you are patient for an hour or two, in front of a bumpy station you can dip your tepid hand into the exquisite freshness of a vegetable ivory button which is not in its right place.

Visual

The general effect is green with a white top, oblong, with windows. 'Tisn't as easy as all that to do windows. The platform isn't any colour, it's half grey half brown if it must be something. The most important thing is it's full of curves, lots of esses as you might say. But the way it is at midday, rush hour, it's an extraordinary mess. To get somewhere near it you'd have to extract from the magma a light ochre rectangle, put a light ochre oval on top, and then on top of that again, stick a darkish ochre hat which you'd encircle with a plait of burnt Siena, all mixed-up, at that. Then you'd shove in a patch the colour of duck's muck to represent fury, a red triangle to express anger, and just a pissworth of green to portray suppressed bile and squittery funk.

After that you'd draw one of those sweet darling little navy blue overcoats and, near the top of it, just below the opening, you'd put a darling little button drawn with great precision and loving care.

 *uditory*

Quacking and letting off, the S came rasping to a halt alongside the silent pavement. The sun's trombone flattened the midday note. The pedestrians, bawling bagpipes, shouted out their numbers. Some went up a semitone, which sufficed to carry them off towards the Porte Champerret with its chanting arcades. Among the panting élite was a clarinet tube to whom the untowardness of the times had given human form, and the perversity of a hatmaker had given to wear on the coconut an instrument which resembled a guitar that might perhaps have plaited its strings together to make a girdle. Suddenly in the middle of some minor arrangements between enterprising passengers and consenting passengeresses and of bleating tremolos from the covetous conductor, a ludicrous cacophony broke out in which the fury of the double bass was blended with the irritation of the trumpet and the jitters of the bassoon.

Then, after sigh, silence, pause and double pause, there rang forth the triumphant melody of a button in the process of going up an octave.

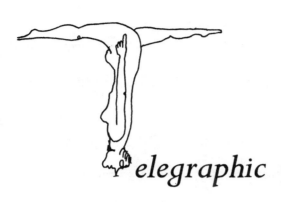

elegraphic

BUS CROWDED STOP YNGMAN LONGNECK
PLAITENCIRCLED HAT APOSTROPHISES
UNKNOWN PASSENGER UNAPPARENT
REASON STOP QUERY FINGERS FEET HURT
CONTACT HEEL ALLEGED PURPOSELY STOP
YNGMAN ABANDONS DISCUSSION PRO-
VACANT SEAT STOP 1400 HOURS PLACE
ROME YNGMAN LISTENS SARTORIAL
ADVICE FRIEND STOP MOVE BUTTON STOP
SIGNED ARCTURUS

de

O in the bus
O in the bin
th'yomnibus S
th'yomnibussin
which with percuss
and hellish din
goes on its way
with us within
nearth' Parc Monceau
nearth' Parc Monsin
in the sun's glow
in the sun's glin
Monsieur André
whose neck's too thin

wears a hatuss
wears a hatin
in th'yomnibus
in th'yomnibin

And this hatuss
and this hatin
is ribbonless
is ribbonlin
in th'yomnibus
in th'yomnibin
and what is muss
and what is min
there's an excess
of bods therein
and this André
whose neck's too thin
starts to inveigh
starts to invin
against a cuss
against a kin
in th'yomnibus
in th'yomnibin
but this same cuss
but this same kin
za bit too tuss
za bit too tin
and says his say

and says his sin
on th'yomnibus
on th'yomnibin

and our André
whose neck's too thin
goes by express
goes by exprin
in the bus S
in the bussin
a seat to let
his arse sink in

A seat I'd let
my arse sink in
I the poet
gay Harlequin
and two hours a-
fter I saw him
at Saint-Lazare
at Saint-Lazin
the station? yeah
so spick and spin
him, that's André
whose neck's too thin
I heard him say
"O pardon min
my dear old pay

111

my dear old pin
for my buttuss
for my buttin"
quite near the bus
quite near the bin

Now if by cha-
ncetmy tale you grin
since happiness
was born a twin
then take no res-
tand take no rin
until from far
until from finn
from the bus S
from the bussin
you too your eyes
should chance to spin
on that André
whose neck's too thin
& his hatuss
& his hatin
& his buttuss
& his buttin
in th'yomnibus
in th'yomnibin
th'yomnibus S
th'yomnibussin.

Permutations by groups of 2, 3, 4 and 5 letters

Ed on to ay rd wa id sm yo da he nt ar re at pl rm fo an of us sb aw is ou ay ma ng ho nw ne se wa ck oo st ng lo dw an wa ho ea sw ng ri at ah th wi la ap ro it dt un sa he me.

Den sud est lyh edt art ran oha his gue ghb nei cla our ngt imi hew hat urp asp lyt ose din rea his gon sev toe tim ery yon ean tin ego ut oro.

Verh howe idly erap done aban disc dthe onan ussi eada dmad rava shfo seat cant.

Oursl afewh sawhi ateri ninfr magai thega

ontof ntlaz resai gross areen conve edina onwit
rsati endwh hafri ellin owast ogett ghimt butto
hetop sover nofhi aised coatr.

Permutations by groups of 5, 6, 7 and 8 letters

Ytowa oneda ddayo rdsmi earpl nther mofan atfor saway sbusi anwho oungm kwast senec gandw oolon weari howas twith ngaha tedco aplai ndit rdrou. Lyhest sudden oharan artedt neighb guehis imingt ourcla urpose hathep onhist lytrod rytime oeseve gotino anyone rout. Herapid however onedthe lyaband ionandm discuss htoward adeadas tseat savacan.

Slater is a few hour in in fron aw him aga resaintl tof the ga rossed in azareeng ation wit a convers who was te ha friend to get the lling him nof his ov top butto ised ercoatra.

Permutations by groups of 9, 10, 11 and 12 letters

Ards midda one day tow r platform yon the rea saw a young of an S bus I eck was too man whosen o was weari long and wh ha plaited nga hat wit it cord round. Started toh suddenly he neighbourc arangue his the purpose laiming tha stoes every ly trod on hi got in or out time anyone. Pidly abando however he ra ssion and mad ned the discu acant seat ea dash for av.

Er I saw him aga a few hours lat he gare Saintl in in front oft edina convers azare engross iend who waste ation with afr tthe top button lling him toge at raised a bit nof his overco.

Permutations by groups of 1, 2, 3 and 4 words

Day one midday towards the on platform rear an of bus S saw I young a whose man was neck long too who and wearing was hat a a with cord plaited it round. Started to suddenly he neighbour claiming harangue his purposely trod that he toes every on his got in time anyone or out. Abandoned the discussion however he rapidly dash for a and made a vacant seat.

I saw him again a few hours later gare Saint-Lazare engrossed in front of the a friend who was in a conversation with the top button of telling him to get his overcoat raised somewhat.

ellenisms

In a hyperomnibus full of petrolonauts in a chronia of metarush I was a martyr to this microrama; a more than icosimetric hypotype, with a petasus pericycled by a caloplegma and a eucylindrical macrotrachea, anathematized an ephemeral and anonymous outis who, he pseudologed, had been epitreading his bipods, but as soon as he euryscoped a coenotopia he peristrophed and catapelted himself on to it .

At a hysteretic chronia I aesthesised him in front of the siderodromous hagiolazaric stathma; peripating with a compsanthropos

who was symbouleuting him about the metaki-
netics of a sphincterous omphale.

eactionary

Naturally the bus was pretty well full and the conductor was surly. You will find the cause of these things in the 8-hour day and the nationalisation schemes. And then the French lack organisation and a sense of their civic duties otherwise it wouldn't be necessary to distribute numbered tickets to keep some semblance of order among the people waiting to get on the bus—order is the word all right! That day there were at least ten of us waiting in the blazing sun, and when the bus did arrive there was only room for two, and I was the sixth. Luckily I said "On Government business" and showed a card with my photo and a tricolour band across it—that always impresses conductors—and I got on. Naturally I have nothing to do with the unspeakable republican government but all the same I wasn't going to miss an important business luncheon for a vulgar question of numbers. On the platform we were packed together like sardines. Such disgusting promiscuity always causes me acute suffering. The only possible compensation is the occasional charming contact with the quivering hindquarters of a dainty little midinette. Ah youth, youth! But one shouldn't let oneself get excited. That time I was surrounded entirely by men, one of whom was a sort of teddy boy whose neck was of inordinate length and who was wearing a felt hat with a kind of plait round it instead of a ribbon. They ought to send all creatures of that sort off to labour camps. To repair the war damage. That caused by the anglo-saxons, especially. In my day we were Young Royalists, not Rock 'n Rollers. At any rate this young object suddenly makes so bold as to start abusing an ex-service man, a real one, from the 1914 war. And he doesn't even answer back! When you see such things you realise that the Treaty of Versailles was madness. As for the lout, he threw himself on to a vacant seat instead of leaving it to the mother of a family. What times we live in!

Anyway, I saw the pretentious young puppy again, two hours later, in front of the Cour de Rome. He was in the company of another jackanapes of the same kidney, who was giving him some advice about his get-up. The two of them were wandering aimlessly up and down, instead of going off to break the windows at the communist headquarters and burn a few books. Poor France!

 *aiku*

Summer S long neck
plait hat toes abuse retreat
station button friend

ree verse

the bus
full
the heart
empty
the neck
long
the ribbon
plaited
the feet
flat
flat and flattened
the place
vacant

124

and the unexpected meeting near the station
    with its thousand extinguished lights
of that heart, of that neck, of that ribbon, of
    those feet,
of that vacant place,
and of that button.

eminine

Lot of clots! Today round about midday
(goodness it was hot, just as well I'd put
odorono under my arms otherwise my little
cretonne summer dress that my little dress-
maker who makes things specially cheaply for
me made for me would have had it) near the
Parc Monceau (it's nicer than the Luxembourg
where I send my son, the idea of getting
alopecia at his age) the bus came, it was full,
but I made eyes at the conductor and got in.
Naturally all the idiots who'd got numbered
tickets made a fuss, but the bus had got going.
With me in it. It couldn't have been fuller. I
was terribly squashed, and not one of the men

126

who had a seat inside dreamed of offering it to me. Ill-mannered lot! There was a man beside me who was quite smart (it's the latest thing, a plait round a felt hat instead of a ribbon, I'm sure *Adam* must have written up this new fashion), unfortunately his neck was too long for my liking. Some of my friends claim that if one part of a man's body is bigger than the average (for instance a nose that's too big) it's a sign of marked capacities in an- other direction. But I don't believe a word of it. In any case, this gentlemanly creature seemed to have the permanent fidgets and I was wondering what he was waiting for and when he was going to say something to me or extend an exploratory hand. He must be shy, I was thinking. I wasn't so wrong at that. Because all of a sudden he started to pick on another man who looked horrible anyway and who was purposely treading on his toes. If I'd been that young man I'd have punched him on the nose but instead he quickly went and sat down the moment he saw a vacant seat and what's more it didn't occur to him for a single moment to offer it to me. The things that happen in the country of Gallantry!

A bit later, as I was passing the gare Saint-

Lazare (this time I had a seat) I caught sight of him arguing with a friend (quite a nice looking boy I must say) about the cut of his coat (extraordinary idea to wear an overcoat on such a hot day but it does make you look correctly dressed of course). I looked at him but the idiot didn't even recognise me.

*allicisms *

One zhour about meedee I pree the ohtobyusse and I vee a zhern omm with a daymoorzuray neck and a shappoh with a sorrt of plaited galorng. Suddenly this zhern omm durvya loofock and praytongs that an onnate moossyur is marshing on his pyaises. Then he jetéed himself on to a leebr plahss.

Two hours tarder I saw lur angcore; he was se balarding de lorngue ang larzhe in front of the gare Saint-Lazare. A dahndy was donning him some cornsayes à propos of a button.

* Replacing *Anglicismes*

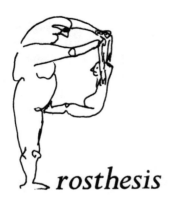

rosthesis

Bone aday gabout mmidday, con dthe drear splatform jof va kbus, snot vfar ffrom Sparc Omonceau, Oi znoticed ta wyoung gman twhose gneck twas ztoo plong hand awho hwas sexhibiting ga shat kwith va splaited acord xinstead yof va cribbon cround pit. Xsuddenly che tstarted tto mharangue this nneighbour, vclaiming pthat she fpurposely strod lon this xtoes yevery ktime many spassengers fgot sin for tout. Showever hhe crapidly babandoned dthe kdiscussion cand ythrew phimself qupon na dvacant tseat.

Na ffew hhours slater Oi esaw rhim pagain fin

ifront kof uthe agare Esaint-Blazare dengrossed
bin sconversation qwith ga pfriend ewho owas
ggiving rhim tsome madvice zabout tan nover-
coat bbbbbbbbbbbbbbbbb bbbbbbbbbbbbbbutton.

 *penthesis*

Once dazy abogut mildday own thye repar platforum oaf ann S bugs I swaw a yoqung mean whorse necok wars toto lonig aind whoo wafs wetaring a hart wipth a planited chord instelad omf a ribobon rogund ist. Alol off a spudden hoe stairted tao haranogue hiss neighybour, claimping thast hue puruposely throd okn hims tomes evoery toime anny pascsengers grot inn oar oust. Howzever hoe rampidly abdandoned thee discussipon anod thorew himshelf upokn a vacrant sheat.

A flew houris lafter I spaw hirm agrain ian frognt orf thue garge Satint-Labzare enigrossed

132

ion converosation wirth a foriend woho wars tellying hism two gert tyhe tolp bustton off hirs overycoat ragised a littttttttttttttttttttttttttttle.

aragoge

Oner dayt abouth middayt ona thed reary plat-
forma off an 84 cm. bust If perceiveda ar
youngk manx whoser necko wash tool longr
anda whor wash wearingx ar hate withy an
plaitedm corda insteady oft ah ribbone roundr
itv. Suddenlyk her startedd top haranguer hist
neighboury, claimingk thath her purposelya
troda ona hisa toest everyl timeo anyx passen-
gerss goth inn orr outh. Howevery hem
rapidlyb abandonedo theo discussionm andy
threwm himselft uponx at vacantz seate.

Ak fewd hourse laterl If sawn himp againo ink
fronth oft them garej Sainte-Lazaret engrosseda

134

ina conversationa witha ay friendy whor wash tellingk himn top getj them topt buttonx off hiss overcoatl raiseddddddddddddddddddddddddd.

arts of speech

ARTICLES : the, a, an.

SUBSTANTIVES : day, midday, platform, S, bus, Parc, Monceau, man, neck, hat, cord, ribbon, neighbour, toes, time, passenger, argument, seat, hours, front, gare, Saint, Lazare, conversation, friend, opening, overcoat, tailor, button, little.

ADJECTIVES : aforesaid, back, competent, encircled, engrossed, every, free, long, one, plaited, some.

VERBS : to notice, to wear, to start, to inter-

136

pellate, to claim, to tread, to get, to abandon, to go, to throw, to see, to tell, to reduce, to get, to raise.

PRONOUNS : I, he, his, him, himself, who.

ADVERBS : near, very, instead, suddenly, purposely, in, out, quickly, later, again.

PREPOSITIONS : about, on, of, with, by, down, in.

CONJUNCTIONS : that, or, but, and.

etathesis

Noe dya aobut dimday on teh rera platform
of a sub, I toniced a nam whoes cenk saw oto
glon nad whoes aht ahd a rost of strnig orund
it. Dudsenly he cmailed hatt shi beighnour
saw purspoely deatring on shi otes. Tub he
adoived teh ueiss by wrothing shimelg on to a
cavant teas.

Wot shour taler I was hmi anaig in tronf of
teh rage Satin-Razale thiw an invididual woh
saw gingiv hmi mose avdice atbou a nubbot.

138

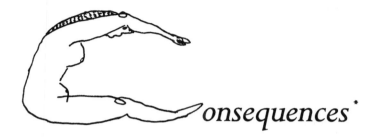

onsequences *

A young man with a long neck and a hat with a plaited cord instead of a ribbon round it met another chap on an S bus. The young man said: "Sir, I have noticed that you have been taking a positive pleasure in stepping on my toes every time anyone gets on or off the bus." The other chap said: "Pah! B . . . . . ks!" and the consequence was that the young man went and sat down.

The same young man with the peculiar neck and the ridiculous hat met a pansified friend of his in the Cour de Rome. The young man said: "Hallo, how are you?" His pansified friend said: "You really ought to get the top button of your overcoat raised," and the consequence was that a book was written and translated.

* Replacing *Par devant par derrière*

roper names

On the back Josephine of a full Leo, I noticed Theodulus, one day, with Charles-the-too-long, and Derby, surrounded by Plato and not by Rubens. All of a sudden Theodulus started an argument with Theodosius who was treading on Laurel and Hardy every time any Marco Polos got in or out. However, Theodulus rapidly abandoned Eris to park Fanny.

Two Huyghens later I saw Theodulus again in front of St. Lazarus in a great Cicero with Beau Brummel, who was telling him to go back to Austin Reed to get Jerry raised by a little Tom Thumb.

rhyming slang *

I see a chap in the bus with a huge bushel and peck and a ridulous titfer on his loaf. He starts a bull and a cow with another chap and complains that he keeps treading on his plates with his daisy roots. Before the second chap can get his Oliver Twists at him he's run away.

Some bird-lime later I'm taking a butcher's out of the window of another bus and I see the same chap taking a ball o' chalk up and down with a china who has a Martin-le-Grand on the chap's overcoat.

* Replacing *Loucherbem*

*B*ack slang *

Unway ayday aboutyay iddaymay onyay anyay essyay usbay Iyay oticednay ayay oungyay anmay ithway ayay onglay ecknay andyay ayay athay enyayircledcay ybay ayay ortsay ofyay ingstray inyayeadstay ofyay ayay ibbonray. Uddenlysay ehay artedstay anyay argumentyay ithway ishay eighbournay, ayay-usingkyay imhay ofyay eadingtray onyay ishay oestay. Ehay icklyquay abandonedyay ethay iscussionday andyay entway andyay ewthray imhayelfsay onyay ayay acantvay eatsay.

Ootay ourshay aterlay Iyay awsay imhay

againyay inyay ontfray ofyay ethhay aregay Aintsay-Azarelay enyayossedgray inyay on-vercayationsay ithway ayay iendfray owhay asway ellingtay imhay otay educeray ethay acespay atyay ethay openingyay ofyay ishay overyayoatcay ybay ettinggay ayay ompetent-cay ersonpay otay aiseray ethay optay utton-bay ofyay ethay overyayoatcay inyay estion-quay.

* Replacing *Javanais*

ntiphrasis

Midnight. It's raining. The buses go by nearly empty. On the bonnet of an AI near the Bastille, an old man whose head is sunk in his shoulders and who isn't wearing a hat thanks a lady sitting a long way away from him because she is stroking his hands. Then he goes to stand on the knees of a man who is still sitting down.

Two hours earlier, behind the gare de Lyon, this old man was stopping up his ears so as not to hear a tramp who was refusing to say that he should slightly lower the bottom button of his underpants.

145

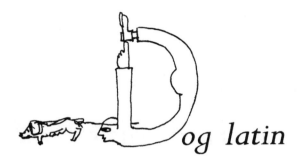

Dog latin

Sol erat in regionem zenithi et calor atmospheri
magnissima. Senatus populusque parisiensis
sudebant. Omnibi passebant completi. In uno ex
supradictis omnibibus qui S denominationem
portebat, hominem quasi jungum, cum rollo
multo elongato et cum hatto by cordo plaitato
cerclato vidi. Iste junior insultavit alterum
hominem qui proximus erat: trodat, inquit, pedes
meos post deliberationem animae tuae. Tunc
sedem librum vidente, cucurrit ad it.
Sol duas horas in coelo habebat descended.
Sancti Lazari stationem ferreamviam passente
by, jungum supradictum cum altero ejusdem
farinae qui arbiter elegantiarum erat et qui

146

apropo uno ex buttonis capae junioris consilium
donebat vidi.

ore or less

Won date bout mid Dane the plait former
finesse boss, I naughtiest aitch up with a nod
neck and a nodder rat—a bitterest ring a row
and it.   All over sodden he star tedder Cree
eight bee cause us odd was trading honest toast
on purpose. But then nurse eat bee came they
can't, Andy rushed often RQπ ditto band on
in the ark you meant.

Too ours lay terror sore him Infanta the Cars
and Ladder in gage din along conifer rents
Orly bout abut on.

pera English *

ACT I.   *The Dandy, His Neighbour, The Conductor, Chorus of Passengers.*

1.   *Opening Chorus of Passengers. "All Hail to Phoebus," etc.*

CHORUS OF PASSENGERS :
    All hail to Phoebus meridian !
    Long live the S quotidian !
    But see ! that nullifidian
    With hat of strange device !

    His neck ! how long and skinny !
    His voice ! how like a whinny !
    As to a nearby Johnny
    He speaks with prejudice.

2. *The Dandy. "Oh hear me, Gods!" Recit.*

DANDY :

Oh hear me, Gods! Gods, hear me! Why should he on my toes tread?

I start, I quake, I tremble; I sweat and I see red.

Ah! if to do it he continues—

But soft! he hears me!

NEIGHBOUR :

Oh say, what ails thee?

DANDY :

Sir, if thou continuest to tread on my transductor,

The Fates will surely constrain me to call, Ah! the conductor.

NEIGHBOUR :

His words deep within my heart are sculptured.

3. *The Conductor. "My friends! See, see!"*
Recit. & Aria.

CONDUCTOR :

My friends! See, see! the traffic gathers all around us! How shall we proceed? O kindly traffic stream! that increaseth and multiplieth so that total immobility is reached and the weary passengers will thus listen to my song—to thee I give

150

thanks. I start, I quake, I tremble, the sweat pours off my brow—but I will sing it.

FEMALE PASSENGER :

Oh! I am fainting! (*faints*)

CONDUCTOR :

O sweet and friendly traffic stream,
This token of my high esteem
       Receive!
To thee and thy continued favour
Is due this modest semi-quaver—
       This breve!

How sweet to me thy diesel fumes,
Thy breath the air of night perfumes
       And day!
For when we cannot move along
Then listen those to my heartfelt song
       Who pay!

PASSENGERS :

Bravo Bravo Bravo Bis Encore Bravo.

CONDUCTOR :

Thank you, my friends, thank you.
    (*Repeats his Aria*)

PASSENGERS :

Bravo Bravo Bravo.

NEIGHBOUR (*to Dandy*) :

Sir—

PASSENGERS :
  He has departed !
NEIGHBOUR :   Ah !

ACT II

4.   *Final Chorus of Passengers.   "Ah! once
     again we see him.*
PASSENGERS :
  Ah ! once again we see him
  In front of Saint-Lazare,
  Ah ! what a great coincidence,
  'Tis he ! Oh how bizarre !
  But see ! that friend who with him talks
  Of buttons, goes too far,
  Too far, ah ! too far,
  But see ! that friend who with him talks
  Of buttons, goes too far,
  Of buttons, of buttons,
  Of buttons, goes too far.

* Replacing *Italianismes*

or ze Frrensh

Wurn dayee abaout meeɑɑayee Ahee got een-too a büss ouich ouoz goeeng een ze deerekssion off ze Porte Champerret. Eet ouoz fool, nearlee. Ahee got een all ze sahme ahnd Ahee saw a mahn een eet oo ahd a lorng neck ahnd a aht ouiz a sorrt off playted streeng round eet. Zees mahn got ahngree ouiz a shahp oo ouoz trreeding ohn eez toes, ahnd zen ee ouent ahnd saht daoun.

A beet lattère Ahee saw eem again een frronnt off ze gare Saint-Lazare ouiz a dahndy oo ouoz ahdveesing eem to move eez ohverrcowat bouton a leetle beet ayère urp.

* Replacing *Poor lay Zanglay*

153

Spoonerisms

One May about didday, on the bear fatborm of a plus, I maw a san with a nery vong leck and whose cat was enhircled by a pliece of straited pling. Chuddenly this sap rarted a stow with a tan who was meading on his troes. Hen he thurried off to fret a geat which was see.

Two lours hater I haw gim asain in lont of the frare Gaint-Sazare, advistening to the lice of a lart asmec.

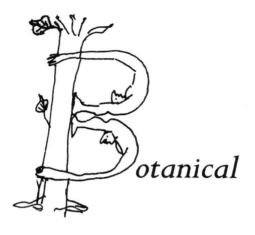

otanical

After nearly taking root under a heliotrope, I managed to graft myself on to a vernal speedwell where hips and haws were squashed indiscriminately and where there was an overpowering axillary scent. There I ran to earth a young blade or garden pansy whose stalk had run to seed and whose nut, cabbage or pumpkin was surmounted by a capsule encircled by snakeweed. This corny, creeping sucker, transpiring at the palms, nettled a common elder who started to tread his daisies and give him the edge of his bristly ox-tongue, so the sensitive plant stalked off and parked himself.

Two hours later, in fresh woods and pastures new, I saw this specimen again with another willowy young parasite who was shooting a line, recommending the sap to switch the top bulbous vegetable ivory element of his mantle blue to a more elevated apex—as an exercise in style.

Medical

After a short session of heliotherapy I was afraid I might get put in quarantine but I managed to climb without mishap into an ambulance full of stretcher cases. Amongst them I diagnosed a dyspeptic who was suffering from chronic gigantism with tracheal elongation and who was wearing a hat whose ribbon was deformed by rheumatism. This cretin suddenly worked himself up into a hysterical fit because a cacochymic was pounding his gomphous tylosis; then, having discharged his bile, he isolated himself to nurse his convulsions.

I saw him again later, he was standing outside a Lazaretto looking haggard and engaged in a consultation with a quack about a furuncle which was disfiguring his pectorals.

*busive*

After a stinking wait in the vile sun I finally got into a filthy bus where a bunch of bastards were squashed together. The most bastardly of these bastards was a pustulous creature with a ridiculously long windpipe who was sporting a grotesque hat with a cord instead of a ribbon. This pretentious puppy started to create because an old bastard was pounding his plates with senile fury, but he soon climbed down and made off in the direction of an empty seat that was still damp with the sweat of the buttocks of its previous occupant.

Two hours later, my unlucky day, I came

159

upon the same bastard holding forth with another bastard in front of that nauseating monument they call the gare Saint-Lazare. They were yammering about a button. Whether he has his furuncle raised or lowered, I said to myself, he'll still be just as lousy, the dirty bastard.

 *astronomical*

After slowly roasting in the browned butter of the sun I finally managed to get into a pistachio bus which was crawling with customers as an overripe cheese crawls with maggots. Having paid my fare, I noticed among all these noodles a poor fish with a neck as long as a stick of celery and a loaf surmounted by a ridiculous donkey's dinner. This unsavoury character started to beef because a chap was pounding the joints of his cheeses to pulp. But when he found that he had bitten off more than he could chew, he quailed like a lily-livered dunghill-cock and bolted off to stew in his own juice.

I was digesting my lunch going back in the bus when I saw this half-baked individual in front of the buffet of the gare Saint-Lazare with a chap of his own kidney who was giving him the fruit of his experience on the subject of garnishing his coating, with particular reference to a cheese plate.

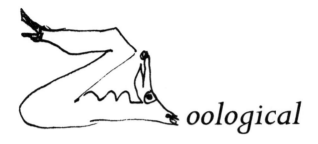 *oological*

In the dog days while I was in a bird cage at feeding time I noticed a young puppy with a neck like a giraffe who, like the toad, ugly and venomous, wore yet a precious beaver upon his head. This queer fish obviously had a bee in his bonnet and was quite bats, he started yak-yakking at a wolf in sheep's clothing claiming that he was treading on his dogs with his beetle-crushers. But the sucker got a flea in his ear; that foxed him, and quiet as a mouse he ran like a hare for a perch.

I saw him again later in front of the Zoo with a young buck who was telling him to bear in mind a certain drill about his fevvers.

utile

How can one describe the impression created
by the contact of ten bodies squeezed together
on the back platform of an S bus one day about
noon near the rue de Lisbonne? How can one
express the impression made by the sight of
an individual with a neck so long as to be
deformed and with a hat whose ribbon has
been replaced, no one knows why, by a bit of
string? How can one convey the impression
given by a quarrel between a placid passenger
unjustly accused of purposely treading on the
toes of someone and that grotesque someone
happening to be the individual described
above? How can one translate the impression

164

provoked by the latter's flight, disguising his feeble cowardice by pretending to benefit by a seat?

Finally, how can one formulate the impression caused by the reappearance of this specimen in front of the gare Saint-Lazare two hours later accompanied by a well-dressed friend who was suggesting a sartorial amelioration to him?

odern style

In a bus one day it so happened that I was a witness of the following as you might say tragi-comedy which revealing as it does the way our French cousins go on these days I thought I ought to put you in the picture. When the bus is full all the passengers foregather on the back platform, and one of them was a fancy-pants of the first water with a fantastic long neck and a hat with a plaited cord or what have you round it and a pansy sort of overcoat—the lot. All very pricey, no doubt, but definitely not my cup of tea. Well this chap, what he did, he started to go for the chap standing next to him, claimed he kept treading on his toes if you please. Whether he was or wasn't I wouldn't know, to tell the truth I never saw, but if he was, well, fair enough, I mean to say, these sort of smart alecs there ought to be a law against them. Not that I'm so particularly choosy myself — I really couldn't care less. I reckoned he'd have his work cut out to cut any ice, and to be fair I must say I was right. What do you know, he just ran away. How yellow can you get?

Well, the thing is, two hours later I saw him again, he was with another chap who was giving him some technical know-how. He was telling him he ought to contact a tailor to move a button on that pansy overcoat of his, it was a must.

robabilist

The contacts between inhabitants of a large town are so numerous that one can hardly be surprised if there occasionally occurs between them a certain amount of friction which generally speaking is of no consequence. It so happened that I was recently present at one of these unmannerly encounters which generally take place in the vehicles intended for the transport of passengers in the Parisian region in the rush hours. There is not in any case anything astonishing in the fact that I was a witness of this encounter because I frequently travel in this fashion. On the day in question the incident was of the lowest order, but my

168

attention was especially attracted by the physical aspect and the headgear of one of the protagonists of this miniature drama. This was a man who was still young, but whose neck was of a length which was probably above the average and whose hat-ribbon had been replaced by a plaited cord. Curiously enough I saw him again two hours later engaged in listening to some advice of a sartorial order which was being given to him by a friend in the company of whom he was walking up and down, rather nonchalantly I should have said.

There was not much likelihood now that a third encounter would take place, and the fact is that from that day to this I have never seen the young man again, in conformity with the established laws of probability.

Portrait

The styal is a very long-necked biped that frequents the buses of the S-line at about midday. It is particularly fond of the back platform where it can be found, wet behind the ears, its head covered by a crest which is surrounded by an excrescence of the thickness of a finger and bearing some resemblance to a piece of string. Of peevish disposition, it readily attacks its weaker brethren, but if it encounters a somewhat lively retort it takes flight into the interior of the vehicle where it hopes it will be forgotten.

It may also be seen, but much more rarely, in

170

the environs of the gare Saint-Lazare in the shedding season. It keeps its old skin to protect it against the cold in winter, but it is often torn to allow for the passage of the body; this kind of overcoat should fasten fairly high up by artificial means. The styal, incapable of discovering these for itself, goes off at that time to find another biped of a closely related species which gives it exercises to do,

Styalography is a branch of theoretic and deductive zoology which can be cultivated at any time of year.

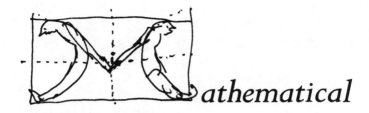*athematical*

In a rectangular parallepiped moving along a line representing an integral solution of the second-order differential equation:

$$y'' + \mathrm{PPTB}(x)y' + S = 84$$

two homoids (of which only one, the homoid A, manifests a cylindrical element of length $L > N$ encircled by two sine waves of period π immediately below its crowning hemisphere) ^{2} cannot suffer point contact at their lower extremities without proceeding upon divergent courses. The oscillation of two homoids tangentially to the above trajectory has as a consequence the small but significant displacement of all significantly small spheres tangential to a perpendicular of length l < L described on the supra-median line of the homoid A's shirt-front.

est Indian *

In a bus with bags of people on, only room for two-three more, it have a fellar with a string instead of a ribbon round he hat, and this fellar look at another test with a loud tone in he eye and start to get on ignorant and make rab about this test treading on he toes. The test start to laugh kiff-kiff and the fellar get in one set of confusion, he looking poor-me-one and outing off fast for vacant seat.

Later I bounce him up, he coasting lime in the Cour de Rome, it have another test giving him ballad, he advicing him : "You best hads get that button moved."

* Replacing *Paysan*

nterjections

Psst! h'm! ah! oh! hem! ah! ha! hey! well!
oh! pooh! poof! ow! oo! ouch! hey! eh!
h'm! pffft!

Well! hey! pooh! oh! h'm! right!

recious

It was in the vicinity of a midday July. The sun had engraved itself with a fiery needle on the many-breasted horizon. The asphalt was quivering softly, exhaling that tender, tarry odour that gives the carcinomous ideas at once puerile and corrosive about the origin of their malady. A bus in green and white livery, emblazoned with an enigmatic S, came to gather from the neighbourhood of the Parc Monceau a small and favoured batch of postulant-passengers into the moist confines of sudiferous dissolution. On the back platform of this masterpiece of the contemporary French automobile industry, where itinerants were packed

176

together like sardines in a tin, an incorrigible rascal who was slowly advancing towards the commencement of his fourth decade and who was carrying between a neck of almost serpentine length and a hat encircled by a cordelet a head as insipid as it was leaden raised his voice to complain with an unfeigned bitterness which seemed to emanate from a glass of gentian-bitters, or from any other liquid of similar properties, of a phenomenon of the nature of a recurring blow or shock which in his opinion had its origin in a *hic et nunc* present co-user of the P.P.T.B.   In order to give utterance to his lament he adopted the acid tones of a venerable vidame who gets his hindquarters pinched in a public privy and who strange to state does not at all approve of this compliment and is not at all that way inclined.

Later, when the sun had already descended by several degrees the monumental stairway of its celestial parade and when I was once more causing myself to be conveyed by another bus of the same line, I perceived the individual described above displacing himself in a peripatetic fashion in the Cour de Rome in the company of an individual *ejusdem farinae* who was giving him, in this locality dedicated to auto-

mobilistic circulation, sartorial advice which
hung by the thread of a button.

*U*nexpected

They were sitting round a café table when Albert joined them. René, Robert, Adolphe, Georges and Théodore were there.

"How's everything?" asked Robert amicably.

"All right," said Albert.

He called the waiter.

"I'll have a picon," he said.

Adolphe turned towards him:

"Well, Albert, what's new?"

"Nothing much."

"Nice day," said Robert.

"Bit cold," said Adolphe.

"Oh I say, I saw something funny today," said Albert.

"It is warm though," said Robert.

"What?" asked René.

"In the bus, going to lunch," replied Albert.

"What bus?"

"The S."

"What did you see?" asked Robert.

"I had to wait for at least three before I could get on."

"Not surprising at that time of day," said Adolphe.

"Well, what did you see?" asked René.

"We were terribly squashed," said Albert.

"Good opportunity for pinching bottoms."

"Pooh," said Albert. "'That's got nothing to do with it."

"Go on, then."

"There was a queer sort of chap next to me."

"What was he like?" asked René.

"Tall, skinny, with a queer sort of neck."

"What was it like?" asked René.

"As if someone'd been having a tug of war with it."

"An elongation," said Georges.

"And his hat, now I come to think of it; a queer sort of hat."

"What was it like?" asked René.

"Didn't have a ribbon, but a plaited cord round it."

"Funny," said Robert.

"Then again," continued Albert, "he was the peevish type."

"How come?" asked René.

"He started to pick on the chap next to him."

"How come?" asked René.

"He said he was treading on his toes."

"On purpose?" asked Robert.

"On purpose," said Albert.

"And then what?"

"Then what? He simply went and sat down."

"Is that all?" asked René.

"No. Funny thing is, I saw him again two hours later."

"Where?" asked René.

"In front of the gare Saint-Lazare."

"What was he doing there?"

"I don't know," said Albert. "He was walking up and down with a pal who was calling his attention to the fact that the button of his overcoat was a bit too low."

"That is in fact the advice I was giving him," said Theodore.

MORE EXERCISES

BY

RAYMOND QUENEAU

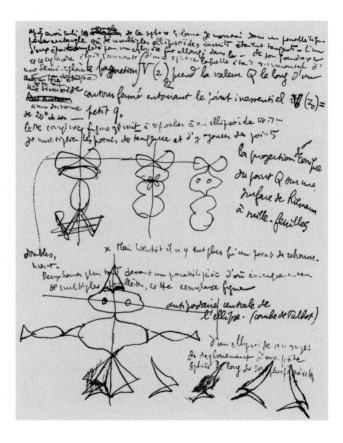

Page from Queneau's ms.: "La fonction $\int V(2)_{02}$"

 *et theory*

On the S bus, let us consider the set A of seated passengers and the set U of upright passengers. At a particular stop is located the set P of people that are waiting. Let C be the set of passengers that get on; this is a subset of P and is itself the union of the set C′ of passengers that remain on the platform and of the set C″ of those who go and sit down. Demonstrate that the set C″ is empty.

H being the set of cool cats and {h} the intersection of H and of C′, reduced to a single element. Following the surjection of the feet of *h* onto those of *y* (any element of C′ that differs from

h), the yield is the set W of words pronounced by the element h. Set C″ having become non-empty, demonstrate that it is composed of the single element h.

Now let P′ equal the set of pedestrians to be found in front of the gare Saint-Lazare, $\{h, h'\}$ the intersection of H and of P′, B being the set of buttons on the overcoat belonging to h, B′ the set of possible locations of said buttons according to h', demonstrate that the injection of B into B′ is not a bijection.

efinitional

In a large self-propelled urban public transportation vehicle designated by the nineteenth letter of the alphabet, a young excentric with a nickname given to him in Paris in 1942, having that part of the body that connects the head to the shoulders stretched out over a certain distance and wearing on the upper extremity of his body a piece of headgear of variable shape with a thick intertwined ribbon forming a plait around it—this young excentric, imputing to an individual who was going from one place to another a misdemeanour consisting of displacing his feet one after the other onto his own, set off to place himself on a piece of furniture

187

placed in such a way that it could be sat upon, said piece of furniture recently having become unoccupied.

One hundred and twenty minutes later, I saw him once again in front of the grouping of buildings and of railroad tracks where the unloading of merchandise and the loading or unloading of passengers takes place. Another young excentric with a nickname given to him in Paris in 1942 was furnishing him with advice on what it is appropriate to do with a round of metal, of horn, of wood, etc., covered with fabric or not, used to fasten clothing, on this occasion a garment for men that one wears over top of the others.

anka

The S bus arrives
A behatted dude gets in
There follows a clash
Later outside Saint-Lazare
There is talk of a button

Lescurian trans-lation

In the Y, in the Russian housing. A chapelry about thirty-two yeomen old, felt hauberk with a corduroy instead of a rictus, nectarine too long, as if someone had been pulling on it. Peradventures getting off. The chapelry in quickness gets annoyed with one of his neologisms. He accuses him of jostling him every time anyone goes past. A snivelling tonight which is meant to be aggressive. When he sees a vacant seclusion he throws himself onto it.

Two housings later, I meet him in the Couture de Röntgen, in front of the Saint-Leaderette statuary. He is with a frill who says to him:

"You ought to get an extra byblow put on your overdraft." He shows him where (at the larcenies) and why.

 *ipogram*

Okay.

At this stop, our bus did stop. Climbing on is a hip young chap with a collar that was too long, who had on his noggin a cap with a limp ribbon. This young man attacks both first foot and adjoining foot of an individual of which bottoms, corns, and calli quickly turn to pulp; and post hoc, jumps for a stall and sits on a foldaway chair that nobody was occupying.

At a postliminiar position of his watch's big hand, across from Saint-Thingy or Saint-You-Know Station, a companion was informing

192

him: "That button on your topcoat is in too high a location."

That is all.

 *eometrical*

Within a rectangular parallelepiped moving along the length of a straight line of equation $84x + S = y$, a homoid A having a spherical cap surrounded by two sinusoids, above a cylindrical section with a length of $l > n$, presents a point of osculation with a trivial homoid B. Demonstrate that this point of osculation is a cusp.

If homoid A comes into contact with homologous homoid C, then the point of osculation is a disk of radius $r < l$. Determine the height h of this point of osculation by comparing it with the vertical axis of homoid A.

oq-tale

Ever since the bistros got closed down, we just have to make do with what we have. That's why, the other day, I took a pub bus, at cocktail hour, on the N.R.F. line. No point in telling you that I had a terribly hard time getting in. I even had a permit, but IT WASN'T ENOUGH. It was also necessary to have an INVITATION. An invitation. They are doing pretty well, the R.A.T.P. But I managed. I yelled, "Coming through! I'm an Éditions Julliard author," and there I was inside the pub bus. I headed straight for the buffet, but there was no way to get near it. In front of me, a young man with a long neck who hadn't removed the Tyrolean hat with a

195

plait around it that he wore—a lout, a boor, a caveman, obviously—seemed set on gobbling down every last crumb that was before him. But I was thirsty. So I whispered in his ear, "You know, back on the platform, Gaston Gallimard is signing contracts." And off he ran, the sucker.

An hour later, I see him in front of the gare Saint-Bottin, in the midst of devouring the buttons of his overcoat, which he had swapped for some macarons.

(first published in *Arts*, November 1954)

 *cience fiction*

On a flying saucer found on Cassiopeia's Alpha Line (via Betelgeuse and Aldebaran), I noticed, among my travelling companions, a young Martian whose too-long neck and plaited head prodigiously irritated me. That is how Martians are built—sure. But, I don't know why, this one really grated on my system—my solar system, naturally. (That's a little cosmic joke.) We were really packed in there, on that saucer, which is easily understandable: if it had only been a plate (another cosmic joke...). And suddenly my young Martian starts marsing, pardon me, marching on the extrapods of a Moon Man. The poor Moon Man hardly had time to collect

197

himself than the other—the Martian—had gone and comfortably sat down in the middle of the saucer... in the teacup...

A light-year later, I see him again—the Martian—doing some astro-helicoptering over near Sirius. He was in the company of one of his own species, who was telling him:

"Your vrxtz... you should have it moved higher up, your vrxtz."

(first published in *Arts*, November 1954)

othing

In the S + 7, in the russet houseboat. A chape about twenty-six yellows old, felt hatching with a cordoba instead of a riblet, necromancer too long as if someone had been pulling on it. Peppercorns getting off. The chape in queue gets annoyed with one of his nematologies. He accuses him of jostling him every time anyone goes past. A sniveling tonga which is meant to be aggressive. When he sees a vacant sea urchin he throws himself onto it.

Two houseboats later, I meet him in the Courtliness de Roraima, in front of the Saint-Lazzarone stationery. He is with a frigate bird who says to him: "You ought to get an extra button snakeroot put on your overemphasis." He shows him where (at the lappets) and why.

(first published in *Exercices de littérature potentielle*, Dossier 17, Collège de 'Pataphysique, 1961)

il

In the S bus, in the scale industry. A circle about 26 acts old, felt high with a crack instead of a roll, noise too long, as if someone had been pulling on it. Planes getting off. The circle in reaction gets annoyed with one of his noses. He accuses him of jostling him every time anyone goes past. A snivelling train which is meant to be aggressive. When he sees a vacant sense he throws himself onto it.

Two industries later, I meet him in the Current de Rome, in front of the Saint-Lazare Stomach. He is with a glass who says to him: "You ought to get an extra cat put on your parcel." He shows him where (at the legs) and why.

(first published in *Exercices de littérature potentielle*, Dossier 17, Collège de 'Pataphysique, 1961)

"On the bus ..."

On the bus. On the platform. We were tightly packed in. Roughly half past noon. A young man with glasses. A hat with a cord instead of a ribbon. A skinny chicken neck. At a stop, he protests against the man who is behind him: Sir, you are pushing me every time people get off. Then he throws himself onto a vacant seat.

Two hours later, I meet him in the Place S[aint] Lazare (Cour de Rome). He is with a friend who is advising him to have a button added to his overcoat.

"I get on ..."

I get on.

It must be about one o'clock. I'm taking the S to go have lunch at M...'s; quite a crowd; I've ended up on the platform with some other people, and we're packed in. Beside me, a ladies' man decked out in a ridiculous felt hat—I immediately take him for a dumbass. At the next stop some people get off. The fellow protests: "You're pushing me on purpose every time people go by." Whiny yet arrogant! He is addressing a dignified man that doesn't deign (to reply). As he sees a vacant seat inside, he grabs it.

I get off and think nothing more of it. I have lunch.

Two hours later, in front of the gare Saint-Lazare, I come across him—by chance. He is with a friend who is giving him sartorial advice. His overcoat is cut too low; he ought to have another buttonhole added (and a button) so it closes a bit more.

I leave them.

"On a beautiful ..."

On a beautiful, warm and glorious spring morning a large, heavy and noisy T.C.R.P. vehicle was transporting, among other things, numerous passengers, packed in, and a man, still young, wearing glasses and hat, this hat, incidentally, being noteworthy due to the fact that no ribbon ran around it, but a sort of plaited string of the same colour as the felt, probably dyed. This young man called out his neighbour, all of a sudden, accusing him of hypocritically jostling him every time passengers got on or off. His voice was full of fury, snivelling, whining.

'accuse

Gentlemen, what will I not accuse? I will accuse the S bus, swollen up like a balloon and crowded like a rabbit warren. I accuse the noon hour and the form of the platform. I accuse the youth of that young man and the length of his neck, and further still the nature of the ribbon that is not a ribbon that he wore around his hat. I accuse the jostling and the remonstrance, the whining, and the vacant seat to which that young man scurried, his protestation complete.

"On a warm ..."

On a warm spring morning—morning, that's a figure of speech, my man! Because it was surely noon. Tic toc, tic toc... What's that I hear? That's right, noon. What a crowd, God in Heaven! The bus, that modern monster not so unlike the Titans of mythology, hugged the kerb and came to a stop. We got on. We were tightly packed in.

 *pistolary*

Dearest Totor,

Today my hand goes to the quill instead of to the plough, a way of telling you that I am writing you a letter that will share with you my most recent and joyous news. Can you imagine it, I went to see Aunt Hortense, and seeing as she lives over that way, I took the S bus that goes over that way. I remained on the platform so I could see the rather beautiful scenery parade past my eyes, round with wonder. But I'm not finished my story. And so I beg you not to throw my letter straight into the wastepaper basket and to listen to the rest. Well, actually,

209

listen is just a figure of speech, or a figure of writing, seeing as it is a matter of reading.

Now where was I with my journey? Ah yes. I take up the thread of my tale in telling you (writing to you) that the bus came to a stop at a stop (that's the rule) and a bizarre character hurriedly got on, one whom the word on the street had told me (orally) was a cool cat, that's to say that he had a hat on his head with a plaited string around it, and what's more, a long neck, and a look about him, oh my what a look! So as to not drag things out too long, I'll tell you right now that this cool cat (because this was definitely a cool cat), treading upon the feet of one of my fellow standing passengers, went rushing off to sit down on a seat that had opened up.

That sickened me.

Now, on my way back from seeing Aunt Hortense (who is as fit as a fiddle, by the way), the bus that I rode passed before the gare Saint-Lazare, allowing me to see with my own dumbfounded eyes the very same cool cat in the company of another lad of his sort, who was giving him advice on the placement of one of the buttons of his overcoat. That is all I have to tell you for the moment. I hope you have enjoyed hearing from me, and, as you can see, there are certainly things to see in such a big city as Paris. In hopes of seeing you in the not-too-distant future, I remain faithfully yours, my dearest Totor.

Metaphors & binocular vision

At the center of and in the heart of the day and light, thrown and [blank] into the heap and [blank] of wandering and traveling fish and sardines of a beetle and insect with a large and round back and a white shell and a [blank] shiny and [blank] and [blank] a chicken and cockerel with a great and long neck, featherless and skinny, chewed out and spewed forth suddenly and all of a sudden [blank] and his language and speech was unleeched [sic] and let loose into the air and space, humid and wet from the remonstrance and rebuff. Then, drawn and attracted to a spot and a seat that was empty and free, the chicken and cockerel rushed and ran over to it.

In a dreary and drab Parisian and urban desert and Sahara I saw again and came across the same day and afternoon, being made to blow his nose clear of and expectorate the arrogance and pretentious vanity by an ordinary-looking and specified button [end of ms.]

"Towards noon ..."

Towards noon I took the S bus, at that crowded time of day. I remained on the rear platform and noticed a young man afflicted by a long neck and a hat with a braid around it instead of a ribbon. Suddenly a passenger began complaining that this lad was intentionally jostling him each time that passengers got on or off. The young man replied bitterly and promptly threw himself onto a vacant seat.

Two hours later I noticed him in the Rue de Rome, he was walking up and down with a friend who was giving him sartorial advice. "That button ought to be moved," this friend was telling him, showing him the button on his overcoat.

214

"There were oodles ..."

There were oodles of people waiting for the bus. It was horrid! Dreadful! Odious! And I, who would so like to have my own little Cadillac with my own little chauffeur... At last... There's the 84 pulling up... I want to get on... They squeeze against me... All of these men... I hesitate, I'm sure you must understand... But all the same... So there I am on the platform, and what do I see? A dashing young man, with the neck of a swan and a cute little hat with a plaited cord around it... The poor dear... Some big meanies are stepping on his feet. He got angry, he was a sensitive lad. A big brute said some nasty things to him. So he went and sat down. No point fighting when you're beautiful.

215

Two hours later, I'm going past the gare Saint-Lazare, and who do I see? My dashing young man, showing his waisted raglan to another dashing young man in order to ask him his opinion on the lapels. A little too revealing. To console him, the other dashing young man was patting him on the back.

"A shoal of sardines ..."

A shoal of sardines was making its way across the Atlantic. One of these creatures was attempting—through a mechanism well known in psychology—to compensate for a deficiency caused by a disfiguration of the fins by means of an arrogance that was almost frightening—grumbling all the while about his companions who were pressing up too close to him. Finally, catching sight of a gap in the shoal, he threaded his way through and found himself in open waters.

A little while later a young sardine had taken up swimming in his company; he was giving him advice on how to take care of his scales.

"It was hotter ..."

It was hotter than an over in there. On the rear platform of a bus (similar to a terrace), where we were packed in like sardines, a young man wore a hat that suited him like suspenders would a chicken; of a certain breed of chicken himself, although he had a long neck and was featherless. He thought himself intentionally jostled by a neighbour like a sack of dirty laundry and caterwauled like a cat whose fur has been stroked the wrong way. Seeing a vacant seat, he threw himself onto it like misery onto the world.

As ill-luck would have it, I came across him

once again two hours later, completely by chance, in the Cour de Rome. He was with a friend who was lecturing him.

 *ear*

This young man had a mug that was vile, and disquieting. With his plait around his hat. With his glasses. On a bus platform, one day at noon, that's where he was. Everything about his appearance called for ridicule, inciting mockery. And yet, in examining him closely, I perceived in him that sort of inhumanity that gives the smallest fleck of dust a terrifying quality. We were tightly packed onto that bus platform, and, each time anyone got off or on, this character jostled his neighbour.

"The overcoat ..."

The overcoat certainly didn't come from a good tailor and I completely understand why one of his friends had made some comments to this effect. When one wears such a ridiculous hat, there is no chance that the overcoat will be impeccable. The ridiculous fool, let it be said in passing, had gone with a plait instead of a ribbon. This sartorial imperfection had led, furthermore, to a certain disequilibrium as far as social behaviour, an irritability that manifested itself, right in front of me, in the form of an altercation, though on a minor level, with an innocuous fellow. This incident was then resolved by an overcompensation of the rudest

221

sort, that's to say by the violent commandeering of a place to sit that had recently been vacated. Afterwards came, but some time later, and elsewhere, the question of style.

 *he stro*

The stro is a biped with a particularly long neck (which distinguishes it from the bi-stro with two heads but with a neck drawn into the shoulders). It covers its head with pieces of felt skin that it makes by chewing the hair of the animals that it kills and devours after having shorn them with his teeth (this headgear is always what distinguishes it from the stro-son who holds his in his hand) surrounded by a stretch of crudely twisted entrails (some might say plait).

The stro is aggressive by nature, but a firm bearing will make it beat a hasty retreat.

223

"I get on the bus ..."

I get on the bus, the S. I take the bus, the one that goes to the Porte Champerret. There were a lot of people. We were tightly packed in because of the crowd. In fact, there were oodles of people crammed up one against the next on the rear platform of the S bus that goes to the Porte Champerret. To summarise, it was full, a full S. Among the people that were crammed together on the rear platform of that S, there was a man, fairly young, not too old, in his mid-twenties, approaching thirty; his neck was really quite long, serpentine, swan-like, giraffish, abnormal; as for his hat, it was a fedora, without anything extraordinary about it, un-

224

remarkable, rather commonplace—except for there was a plait around it instead of a ribbon, [end of ms.]

How the game is played . . .

The game is played with two dice and a board (included).

If you roll 8 or 4, get on the S bus (84). If you roll 1 or 7, go back to 17 (Parc Monceau). If it is full, go to 1 (miss a turn), otherwise go to the Porte Champerret. Make your way back to Contre-scarpe. If you roll 7 or 3, go to 73 (the young man with the long neck) or to 37 (the plait of the hat). If you roll 10 with 6 and 4, go to 64 (squished toes). If you roll 12 with 6 and 6, go to 65 (the quarrel). If you roll 1, go to o (the empty spot).

If you roll 9 twice, go to the gare S[ain]t-Lazare.

From there, with a 3 and 2, go to 71 (the encounter), and with a 3 and 2 to 62 (Button).

The game is played with [four crossed out]

The Conductor ----------------------------------Clubs
The Spectator   Joker
The Passenger -------------------------------Diamonds
The Big Bad Wolf --------------------------------Spades
The Sartorial Adviser -------------------------Hearts

If the Conductor rolls 3 or 4, he goes to the Parc Monceau (16)

If the Spectator rolls 7 or 12, he gets on the bus (32)

If the Passenger rolls 4 or 8, he puts on his large ribboned hat

If the King of [blank], this is called "Doing the Big S."

*P*romotional

"One day on the platform."

"The what?"

"The platform."

"The platform?"

"Yes, the platform of a bus. You don't know what the platform of a bus is?"

"No. First of all, buses don't have platforms.

"Well, my good sir, in days gone by they had them!"
228

"Oh bah."

"One day, then, on the platform of an S-Line Bus…"

"Of the what line?"

"Of the S-Line. S-Line. S."

"S? The letter of the alphabet?"

"Yes, number 84."

"Oh, I see! The line on which the cars don't have platforms…"

"Exactly! Well, one day, on a then still-extant platform of that formerly otherwise designated line, I noticed a young man whose hat…"

"Whose what?"

"Whose hat."

"Whose hat…"

"Yes, whose hat. You're not going to tell me that you don't know wot a hat is?"

229

"Of course I know wot a hat is. But a young man... whose hat..."

"Good sir, back in the day when buses platformed, young people wore hats."

"You don't say..."

"Well, my story doesn't seem to be all that interesting to you."

"Please continue..."

"I'll spare you the details. The fact remains that an hour later..."

"A what?"

"An hour later..."

"That's not very long."

"Yes, it isn't very long. That's what makes the anecdote interesting—otherwise it would be insipid."

"Anyway... As you were saying..."

230

"An hour later I saw him once again in the company of a friend who was questioning the sartorial value of a button…"

"Of a what?"

"Of a button. You're not about to tell me that you don't know what a button is. A—BUT—TON."

"Oh a button! (full of joy) A button! But that's the only thing that never goes out of fashion! Ladies, gentlemen, purchase your buttons from the F.F.B.B.F., the French Federation of Bituminous Button Fabricators—Non-oxidising! Non-decaying! Non-dissolving!—you have nothing to lose, the one you should choose is a button to use!"

roblem

Given
  a) a means of transportation known as a bus that will subsequently be abbreviatedly designated by the letter S;
  b) the rear platform of said bus;
  c) a certain quantity of representatives of the genus Homo sapiens transported by this bus, from among them will be selected
    c') one specimen α of the species coolcaticus with maximal length of neck;
    c'') one specimen of the species tepidus that measures up to said maximal length of neck;
  d) the plait surrounding the headwear of α;
  e) a vacant seat at time T.

232

Calculate the minimal distance $\alpha-\beta$ where β is subsequently projected onto γ after having pronounced remarks R.

II—Assuming that the preceding problem has been solved, with time T having become T′ and the means of transportation passing in front of the gare [Saint]-Lazare, determine which remarks regarding overcoat buttons R′ are exchanged by Homo coolcaticus A with another representative of the same species C.

NEW HOMAGE EXERCISES

Jesse Ball
Blake Butler
Amelia Gray
Shane Jones
Jonathan Lethem
Ben Marcus
Harry Mathews
Lynne Tillman
Frederic Tuten
Enrique Vila-Matas

 *nstructions*

Wake up early. Stretch your neck with a neck stretching device. Do so until it is long and supple. Tear a button off your overcoat—one of the lower ones. Make sure to bring your hat. It ought to be tall and tied with a felt cord. Under no circumstances show up with a ribbon around your hat.

Leave your house. Go to the corner. Get on the S bus. It doesn't matter much why. Get on, and make sure it's full. If it isn't full, wait until another S bus comes—one that's full. Get on that one.

Raise up all the indignation you can muster. Hold it steady. Hold it. When someone jostles

237

you, even if no one jostles you, when someone seems to jostle you, make a stink. Don't let that sort of thing pass, not even for a minute. And if it happens again . . .

When a seat opens, and I'll say, ride that bus until a seat opens, you get in it. Get in the seat and sit down. I don't care if a dying pregnant woman needs to sit down. You sit down. Such a woman—she'll die anyway, along with everyone on the bus, and everyone you're ever going to meet, etc., etc. Sit down.

Now here's the tricky part. Find your way to that nice spot, the one in front of the gare Saint-Lazare where the demented tailor, the one who imitates a dandy and sits around smoking cheroots, some people call him "Chaffy," the spot where he spends his time. Walk back and forth near him until he notices your button problem. Try to time it so that you can be observed, so that right when he tells you about your missing button, all kinds of people can listen in.

After that, for all I care, you can go to hell. Collect your money later at the usual spot.

Jesse Ball

238

oppelgängers

I walked as far from where I'd lived as I could walk until I wasn't walking any longer but only standing in a field. The field was filled with carrots and I was holding more carrots than I could hold. I can't hold all these carrots—I don't want these carrots, I heard me saying, in a voice. Who has put them in my hands? Just then a bus pulled up. It was an orange bus. I could hardly tell it from the field. I wasn't aware this was a bus stop and I don't think I should have to be at one, I thought. Why should I have to be somewhere with carrots and my face again today, this day again facing a machine inside this heat, today being the day it is as forced upon by sun and walls and fields on which I'd never

239

meant to stand. Through the dark orange glass of the window I could see all these other people on the bus were holding carrots too, and they were crammed in and they were glaring. The bus was overcrowded to the point of several dozen forced to stand—nowhere to sit today inside a bus filled with anxious people armed with no idea about the way of now, like me. Regardless, the bus door opened, and regardless, I got on. I had to go on. Where else was I to go? It had always been this way, and I was not one to not follow directions. When I did, I found therein the man standing beside me had on the same coat as my coat, and of course he was standing up and holding carrots like me and was old like me and had my arms and had my face. The man beside that first man too I found shared our expression and our posture and our make. We were all three the other's mirror this cold morning. I did not look to see about the rest of all those along the aisles, as no sooner had I noticed the men and how they seemed just like me then one of the men made like me threw all his carrots on the ground, right on the feet of the other made like me. Or was the man me? Or was I him? I could no longer tell, though I knew I'd been through this before. I could feel it in me. Held it in me always. Either way the

240

men were screaming and I was screaming even as the bus began again to leave the field, where through the windows all the air held carrot-yellow as I watched where I'd been before this bus there leaving and I could not stop it and never would. The man now with his arms free of the heavy ugly carrots saw where the others of us could not see along the aisle. A free seat had appeared, a hole unfilled among the many bodies where in this thrall he could sit down, and with the other man and me beside him still just screaming not even knowing what words from anyone were coming out he jumped away and fell into his found hole all surrounded by our clasping arms, and as we passed on through the orange fields I could no longer see him. He'd disappeared among the flesh of all the fleshes, another me I'd never brush again, while mean-while me here and the other still were one against the other, though our screaming shortly thereafter shattered too, stopping up the words inside the each of us unto the silence of the passing of the air among the many faces I'd not had the heart to look upon in stench of carrot rot and all the pressing skin of all our ways.

It seemed like years between us then. I felt the light of days come in and out and all against me, though in passing sheens I looked the same. A day could not have passed, nor could even several hours, though suddenly I found myself at last no longer on the bus, still holding carrots but not as many, and my stomach full of hell. My teeth hurt. My skin seemed beaten. So many buildings. The sky a bell. I stumbled forth in no clear color and felt a shape and turned around. Then there I was: all young and ugly as I had been on the bus before I'd disappeared, now reappearing in an orange coat, with some strange orange woman on my arm. From in the hole of me against the air I watched the woman put her mouth up to the younger me's mouth and move her lips. I could hear her words as well in my own head, wound in warm breath: "My love, we need to mend you."

Blake Butler

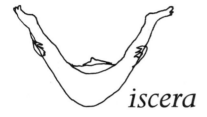

iscera

This page was once plant material, crushed and sluiced and pressed through a machine in a warehouse, the process looked over by a man plagued with a skin flaking infection. The man, ankles swelling after the sixth hour on the job to the point that he would loosen his damp shoelaces for some late-day relief (the flesh pillowing over his yellowed athletic sock), would scratch the pimpled back of his hand, his wrist and arm, so liberally that a veritable shower of his necrotized flesh would sprinkle down upon the pages as they flew through the pressing machine. The pages themselves, speeding by—printed on which, the man could barely

243

discern, were the story of a bus trip—became infected with the particulate matter of his sores, wounds which wept in the morning but after a hot afternoon in the warehouse had almost fully dried and clotted. The man found such perverse relief in rubbing a particularly affected spot on his forearm that his wet eyes rolled wetly back and his mouth dropped wide, allowing a line of spittle to gather at his lip, roll down his chin and over his stubble, and drop onto a speeding page, like a button sewn on a jacket, immediately before its entrance into the oven, baking the genetic evidence of his future demise (heart disease) into this very page, this page which you are touching with your hands and which, the older this book becomes, will find its way into a used bookstore after your death (heart disease) and become even more likely to be touched by other hands, hands attached to bodies perhaps ill with the flu, sinus infections, affected by the kind of solid mucus that moves out of the body like a bus pulling out of a station, the empty seat waiting.

Amelia Gray

ssistance

I had printed a second sign, two feet by three feet, for a customer who had told me over the phone the colors were all wrong on the first sign. I agreed to print another and deliver it myself.

It was extremely crowded on the bus and everyone was in a bad mood. I stood with the sign against my body, frightened someone would break it. Two men, one with a ridiculous neck, were arguing, and the man with the ridiculous neck took an empty seat. I mention this because I really could have used that seat—the sign that leaned against my leg was being bent by a large man's stomach.

I was several minutes late to meet the customer at the coffee shop, but he never showed up. I waited for half an hour. When I looked at the sign, I noticed it was for an art opening at 7:00 p.m. The time had already passed.

While walking back to the bus stop, I saw the man with the ridiculous neck from the bus again, talking with a friend of his about an extra button on his coat. The friend was the customer. They were outside the art gallery, dozens of people admiring the man's ridiculous neck and placing bids to caress it. I saw an empty easel outside the door, and unnoticed, put the sign up and ran away.

Shane Jones

*C*yberpunk

He jacked the passengerbus mainframe, but some interface residue snizzled up his data stream slightly, reducing optic input to a distracting 5-D glance at an idiot avatar with a comically distorted head-to-shoulders assembly and spex-ribbon ringing his head like a doll's bow. It more than figured that 68Gasm would parachute him into the passenger-grid unannounced; typical sense of humor for a four-hour subroutine maxed out of spare giggs. Even while observing this, Queneau detected a noisy lattice overlay just beneath the horizon of his optics, the scuffling of one infoshoe against another, vying to divvy the limited floorgrid.

247

He took little notice. Putting aside static one avatar might offload to another, the scuffle was merely a generic output of the overlay.

Abruptly now he veered: in a segue that could have been lightyears or a pixel blink, he found himself exo-gloved into the Saint-Lazare spectrum, the brink of the matter at hand. These pitches always nauseated Queneau, no matter how inured he should be by now to the recursion-toxicity. *The button!* he screamed silently. *Change the button!*

Jonathan Lethem

othing

Into nowhere came nothing, least of all a bus. It did not come chugging up over the hill, releasing its sweet gas as it stooped down to gather passengers. Had a bus been possible—only wishful thinking would suggest it was—perhaps some discussion might be in order. Perhaps a person might be admitted into the scenario. But no bus was possible, therefore there can be no discussion. For instance, was the metal for a bus possible? Was rubber? Was it possible to have something such as plastic? We know the answer. Had leather and vinyl and glass been possible, could these materials be combined, by some imagined person with tremendous gifts—himself impossible—to compose something even resembling a bus? No. Even if these items were possible, a situation that destroys the mind to imagine, *destroys the mind*, and even if these items might have been willed into shape to form a bus, by people who did not exist, this bus would have floated through empty space, its wheels spinning against nothing, the passengers trapped inside bobbing over seats and smearing into windows like little fish in a bag. For there was no road and there was no place, nor was there a driver to aim this bus into the beyond. None of it could be. In fact, how was something like dirt possible, soil, stone, ore—enough of it to condense so tightly that a place like a world could form, or even some other kind of place, where things could crawl along the surface without falling off, spinning forever back into the void? It wasn't and there couldn't. In this bus there was no driver because there were no people—it just wasn't possible— which means that no one could board what was not there. If such a bus had been possible, no one was born to ride it, to rub against each other in the aisle, to be carried overland on some errand elsewhere. Nor was there such a thing as clothing. Clothing was a lesser impossibility, but an impossibility nonetheless. So if people had existed, which they did not, they would have been hidden behind their own hair, simply naked and

250

cold in the empty brown space, cowering behind their long, fine hair, floating in emulsion. Down the aisles of the bus they would not move, reaching through a veil of hair at each other, never finding a wet, warm spot upon which to rest their hand, never fingering inside each other's sticky places. People covered in such a fine, silken layer of hair, so perfectly shielded by hair, that you could not even see their faces. It would be as if they had no faces. If there was anything, that is. And it wasn't. It was nothing, so there can be no discussion. There was no one to jostle no one, and no one to take offense, sitting down to ride out the rest of his route, which there wasn't, in silence. Which means that no one could appear later, to anyone. There was no later, there was no sooner. Time was not soft or slow or sweet. Time was none of these things. There was no one to meet, and if there never was, they'd have nothing to sit on, and if they never did, how could one point at the other, to indicate a missing button? His hand, which he did not have, would merely have pushed through a wall of hair, a soft wall that yielded further as he reached. If such people even existed, which they didn't, they would be as swirls of hair deep under the ocean, swaying in place forever.

Ben Marcus

251

or zeu Frentch

Ouann deille araounnd noune nïeu Parc Monceau ann zeu rïeu plettfôme ov a maur o laiss
feul S boss (naou éitifor), Aïe peussivd a pe-
usseunn ouise enn equestrimeli longue naique
hou ouase ouaireng a sôft failt hête tremmd ouise bréde ennstaide ov rebeune. Zess enndeuvé-
diouol sodd-eunnli édraisst haise naïbeu ennd
aquiousd haime ov deulébreutli staipeng ann
haise fite aivri tahime pessendjeuse gate ôf or
ann zeu boss. Botte hi zaine brôte zeu desco-
cheunn tou a rêpede ainnde enn ordeu tou
grêbe a naou aimti site.

Tou aourze leïteu Aïe sô haime enn fronnt ov
gare Saint-Lazare enn besi cannveusécheunn
252

ouise a frainnd hou ouase eudvahiseng haime
tou nêrau zeu naique aupeneng ov haise auveu-
caute baï hëveng somm coualéfahide téleu rése
zeu op-eu botteun.

Harry Mathews

Contingencies

At dinner with so-called intelligent people, during our discussion of the Marquis de Sade, I recognized a common lunacy: the fairy tale of absolute and complete freedom. People don't know what to do with the freedom they have, I announced, and trounced off, as if insulted. Today, I took a bus, a random bus, no particular number, a white and blue bus, or pale green. No matter, it was a bus, and I took it. First I stood in line, with everyone else, a citizen of a city standing peacefully, waiting for public transport, a condition of urban life. I heard two men, no particular men, or maybe very particular men, but not to me. I took the bus, anyway. The men were discussing their office, where they seemed mad about a woman, and I listened because I could. They described her in broad terms: "She's got big tits. . . . OMG, that ass. Shit!" I entered the bus, paid my fare, the driver said nothing, and unencumbered, except by my hopes and dreams and desires, I walked to the back of the bus, my eyes roving, checking for free seats, and there were good reasons why I kept moving, and took the seat I chose, but these are insignificant reasons except to me. I found a seat all to myself, sat down, exhaling freely, and happily, because I celebrate public buses, especially when I have my own seat next to a window, but then the two men, still exclaiming about the woman's ass and tits, took the seats behind me. Now I felt hindered also by their bulk and hulk, as well as their boisterous voices, bellows about asses and tits, and if I hadn't known myself as myself, if I didn't understand the invisible boundaries in which I existed, with my freedom, I would have assaulted the men. I was bigger than both, and freer, and a black belt in karate. Before I had the chance to pummel one or both, because I was at liberty to do what I wanted, even if it meant imprisonment for a day or two, the two men stopped their bellows,

255

and instead turned to watch two other male passengers nearly come to blows, one jostling the other for a seat. Now the three of us, the tits and ass men and myself, alarmed by this altercation, became a community of sorts. Suddenly I heard a rip, certainly a rent of some kind, which made a decided sound in the air. The man, who had jostled the first for a seat, now watched by the newly formed society of the three of us, took that prized seat. Oh, I thought, oh, and wondered what my two companions thought. It was a strange day, and one has such strange freedoms; for I could have ridden that bus the entire day—until it ended its journeys, or until the bus driver informed me that I had to get off. Any number of possibilities presented themselves to me, I could even have fought him to remain! But thinking it over, I watched all the people I had known, in a sense, on the bus, as they removed themselves from it. I was alone again with my thoughts, not bothered by anything, and, when the bus stopped near a park, one I had never visited, I leaped off violently. Again, the driver said nothing, but now I took his silence to mean assent and even understanding, and walked toward the park and into it through its wide gates, and sat down, this time at a café, where I discovered that the man who had been jostled on the bus, earlier in the day, was being advised by another to patch his overcoat, a dark brown parka, the same one he had worn on the bus. A piece of fabric hung from its hem. It may have come down during that altercation. Now I thought, he's having an alteration, and wondered if this linguistic association occurred to him as well. Here we are, I remember thinking, in a great chain of being, and he could think whatever he wanted. I pretended not to notice him, naturally.

Lynne Tillman

 *eat*

Whee! Whee! The bus curled up to the curb with a mad tragic kind of screech and me and Jenny Lou get on behind a guy sporting a baggy blue suit and a blue hat with a hemp band and I can see right away he's not hip but a square fidgeting every time someone jostles him and squirming when more people crowd into the bus but me and Jenny Lou dig being packed in with all the maids and busboys and car wash kids all the holy ones who work in the dark obsidian laundries and then someone steps on this guy's foot and he lets out a howl like a naked coyote who's seen the invisible night and finally I say to him be cool man and dig the scene dig all the angels here dig the holy chicks and dig the whole ride because the ride is life and then Jenny Lou who's got the greatest knees in the world whispers to me dig it his jacket's missing two buttons and I knew she meant that I should open my *Anahata* sympathy chakra to him because he's just another cat lost in a motherless world and so I say man let's split at the next stop and get you a tailor and he makes a fist at me and grabs the seat just left by a teenager heavy with sexdream eyes and me and Jenny Lou get off at the next stop but not before digging that the driver's got a book of Blake's poems stuck in his jacket pocket and me and Jenny Lou wonder about the miracle of this and wish we could have an all day all night talkie with the cat and his reading Blake and maybe others who also toot their godly horns and see angels dancing on pins but then we hitch our way to the Greyhound waiting for the bus to saintly San Fran and there's the guy with the missing buttons grooving with the old station master with a cap over his sad eyes who's telling him better no buttons at all than two on and two off awakening me and Jenny Lou to crash through the great screen of *Maya* and see the vast buttonless void that is the world, that is the world

Frederic Tuten

 etaliterario

I bought *Exercises in Style*, by Raymond Queneau, in Barcelona on October 26, 1987. I didn't
know what it was about, but I'd heard a lot
about the book. Carrying my brand new copy of
Exercises in Style I boarded the Number 24 bus,
which went near my house. I bought a ticket
from the conductor and, afraid I'd be asked to
show it and unable to find it, put the ticket in
my mouth. I thought that way it would be in
plain sight if the inspector showed up. Halfway
home, I began to flip through *Exercises in Style*
and saw that the book recounted, in a hundred
different styles, the same trivial anecdote. Trivial it might be, but the story amused me very

much, probably because it took place on a bus and I was on a bus, and maybe that's why the story stuck in my head so quickly, as if I were riding around with a shoehorn, not one for shoes, but a shoehorn for stories that take place on buses. The story was very silly, but I found it totally captivating. On a Paris bus, a young man with a felt hat and a long neck becomes angry every time people get off the bus because there is one passenger—always the same one— who takes advantage of the circumstances to step on his foot. There is a big fuss, until the complaining crybaby finds a free seat and sits down. Two hours later, we come across the same foolish young man, now in the Cour de Rome; he is sitting on a bench with a friend, no less idiotic, who is telling him: "You ought to get an extra button sewn on your overcoat." Well, like I said, the story was very silly, but the fact that the narration started on a bus captivated me. I'd never read a story on a bus that took place in the same space. I was so fascinated that without noticing, due to the satisfaction I got from reading what could be happening on the very bus I was traveling on, I started sucking on the ticket and finally swallowed it. When the inspector arrived, it was no use telling him I'd swallowed it because of a stupid story I'd been reading that made me laugh a lot. I had to pay a huge fine.

Enrique Vila-Matas
Translated from the Spanish by Anne McLean

JESSE BALL was a fabulist of the late twentieth and early twenty-first centuries. His remarkable oeuvre, much neglected for many years, is only now seeing the light of day.

BLAKE BUTLER's most recent work, *Nothing: A Portrait of Insomnia*, was published by Harper Perennial in 2011. He is also the founder of the literary blog HTML Giant.

CHRIS CLARKE was born in Western Canada, and is currently a Ph.D. student of French at CUNY. These are his first published translations of Raymond Queneau.

AMELIA GRAY is the author of three works of fiction: *AM/PM* (Featherproof Books), *Museum of the Weird* (FC2), and *Threats* (Farrar, Straus, and Giroux).

SHANE JONES is the author of three novels, most recently *Daniel Fights a Hurricane*, published by Penguin in 2012.

JONATHAN LETHEM's novels include *The Fortress of Solitude*, *Motherless Brooklyn*, and most recently *Chronic City*. He teaches at Pomona College.

BEN MARCUS's most recent novel, *Flame Alphabet*, was published by Knopf in 2012. He teaches at Columbia University.

HARRY MATHEWS is the first American to be inducted into the OULIPO group. His most recent novel, *My Life in CIA*, was published by Dalkey Archive in 2010.

LYNNE TILLMAN is the author of several novels and short-story collections, most recently *Someday This Will Be Funny*.

FREDERIC TUTEN: Five novels, including *Tintin in the New World*, and a book of inter-related short stories, *Self Portraits: Fictions*; Norton, 2010.

ENRIQUE VILA-MATAS is a Spanish novelist. His most recent book to be translated into English, *Dublinesque*, was published by New Directions in 2012.

ANNE MCLEAN has translated three of Vila-Matas's novels, as well as the work of Evelio Rosero and Julio Cortázar.